THE QUEEN OF WHAT REMAINS

DECADES, VOLUME 2

BRIAN PACINI

ISBN: 978-1-73297-861-4

Cover Art and Design By:

Brigitte Thompson

Instagram: brigitte_thompson_art

The Queen of What Remains

The Queen of What Remains

For Anna—my fierce warrior, my queen

Competing is intense among humans, and within a group, selfish individuals always win. But in contests between groups, groups of altruists always beat groups of selfish individuals.

—E.O. Wilson, *The Social Conquest of Earth*

THIRD STORY

BUCK BREAKING (Continued)

MURDER OF ONE

(Fetien)

❧

I reach up my right sleeve and tug hard on the strap. The silk ribbon slides around my taut body, pulling the branches and twigs flat against my back. My camouflage, the costume Charlotte designed for me, is fitted into form. Leafage, attached from the forest, presses firm against me so I can run, so I can attack, all while concealed.

Vines lace through my kinky hair, wilder now in the wilds of Central Asia. The leafy laurel wraps my head like a halo, protecting me in the same way as the costume, making me hidden and veiled, accentuating my superpower of invisibility.

Blacks, browns, muted earthy colors blend with my "cocoa-butter" skin, blend with my rifle, blend into the earth and forest I quickly glide through now that my costume is pulled firm against my body in attack mode. I dart through the trees, making my way back to the base and today's grand quarry. Sticks snap beneath my feet. Wind dances in my ears, carrying the fluttering sounds of crows shadowing me.

I run through the forest hidden from everyone except the crows. They follow me now, keeping their distance but always around. They even serve as a lookout, pointing out the prey with alerting squawks. When I first noticed them and their warnings, I thought they would give my position away, with their deep-throated ka-kaws. But like me, they are invisible, just part of the scenery. No one notices them either. When they alert me, still ignored by my target, they get their reward, to feed on the bloody little pieces of my destruction. The crows and I have a symbiotic relationship, and we make a formidable hunt.

I reach the edge of the forest and settle into the ground, nestling into the dirt and ground-cover. I slowly pull the strap up my right sleeve and the branches and twigs stand to attention on my back. I scan the surrounding brush and pull the right combination of straps on my chest to match the colors of the forest, more auburn and brown than the green lushness on our side of the river. Charlotte's genius flaunts in this costume, her masterpiece. Hidden between Charlotte's blending bush and the ground, I stay completely still for twenty calming, steadying breaths. After I am sure no one has spotted me, I remove the scope off my rifle and hold it to my right eye, brushing away some wayward leaves from my halo. I scan the old military base, looking for movement, traps, or signs that the new hole I dug under the fence days before has been discovered.

There are no traps, no villains waiting to waylay me. My crows have perched on the fence and make no noise. But the base looks different now that the American soldiers from Afghanistan have taken over. It has changed since we abandoned it, after the Battle of the Base, when we killed the tyrannical National Guard soldiers and escaped into the mountains with Kevin's herd of sheep and any supplies we could carry.

Signs of damage decorate the base. Were they attacked again after we left? Aside from the newly burnt buildings and bullet holes, the compound just looks wrong — tribal, almost, a state of decay continuing to spread even after I dug a small hole under the fence a few days ago.

The electricity is gone; moonlight and torches offer the only light. The tiki torches burn in random patterns and throw a weird uneven illumination. Despite no warning from the crows, I stay hidden and scan the shadows dancing in the light of the fires, looking for any movement or watchers. I patiently look back and forth along all the buildings when I see a human figure deep inside the base, near the flagpole where Michael was whipped and where we burned the dead National Guard soldiers in a huge, gruesome funeral pyre.

The human figure is standing tall with arms raised, but something is off. I focus on the form. Their position is too awkward, too constrained, a Y that doesn't move. By the end of two, still minutes, I know the person is never moving again.

Just beyond, the flagpole stands barren in the courtyard, a long rope dancing in the breeze. No Stars and Stripes blow in the wind. This worries me as much as the crucified figure.

I grit my teeth with resolve. I release the latches and buttons to undo the costume, then slip out of the getup and lay her on the ground on top of my rifle. I mark a nearby tree with a cut of cord and stalk toward the base.

Days before, after I dug the hole under the fence, I went back into the forest in stealth-mode — branches up, body down — to watch the base, hidden and silent. I monitored and timed the guards for three motionless days. I calculated the distance from each guard station and gauged the most opportune time to sneak back into the base. Four AM. Now, before dawn, is the best time.

My pistol rests holstered on my hip. My knife is brandished in my hands. Two grenades bulge on the small of my back. Lengths of cord and rope wrap around me like a big diagonal X across my torso. My crows have launched from the fence and are circling above in anticipation.

I take another look around the darkened base then slide the

scope into my X and move out of the forest. I feel naked without my rifle and costume. My fingers run across the laurel around my head, a quick prayer for protection. I reach the fence and slide through the hole. On the ground still, I imagine Mother Mary next to me, guiding me, protecting me, but it feels wrong, asking for her protection as I seek death. I look to the bastardized, twisted crucifix ruling over the base and the evil within, and remind myself that the death I seek is justified.

THE *FIGURE-Y* HAUNTS my peripheral vision as I sneak my way through the base; it confuses me, an unforeseen variable. Even my crows ignore the haunting mass. I want to investigate, but it does not fit into my calculations. I allotted myself thirty-five seconds to make it to the officers' quarters, and I have no time to study this problem. I tell myself this again and again and keep moving while throwing quick glances at the hanged man near the flagpole.

There is a guard at the door of the officers' quarters, so I go around the outer buildings, out of his sight, to the other side of the barracks. I check my watch. Thirty-three seconds. I climb the steel gutter to the first level. The night fills with a soft pitter-patter as I tiptoe-run across the roof. I jump catty corner to the shelf below the windows that lines the second-story hallway leading to the major's old room. The room where our fallen leader, the commanding officer who congratulated me on my selection into the leadership program, was murdered in her sleep by exhaust from the National Guards' Humvees. The major is buried in a field by the fence, but a new leader occupies her room — not the racist corporal who took over, who we killed and cremated in the Battle of the Base, but the next installment of tribal tyranny. My grand quarry. I will not be killing him in his sleep; I will wake him and let him know who hunts his soldiers in the forest.

With no A/C, no electric fans, the quarters are warm even in the fall weather. They leave the windows cracked open. I take my knife and slice the screen at the bottom, then trace the blade all around the rectangle. I pull the screen down and fold into a square and slip it between my breasts and clothing. The piece of screen can be added to my nest when I sleep to keep bugs away from my face.

I press the knife firm between my lips. I lower the window, then hop into the hallway.

My heart finally starts to race. Calm up until now, there is something evil and eerie about this hallway. I felt it even when I carried the major's body to the big burial hole months before. I am crouched on the floor ready to leap back through the window. Looking down, I listen for any sound. In the moonlight and torches, I can still see a darkened bloodstain underneath my hands and feet. I try to shake the visual of what caused that morbid portrait out of my mind, probably from when Kevin, Michael, and Eva split off and attacked the racist National Guard leaders during the Battle of the Base.

I look to the door and take a deep breath as I stand up and walk toward it. I remove the knife from my mouth and pull the key out of my pocket with my other hand. I step to the door and wait a few seconds, listening for any sounds, for any pique of my subconscious that something is wrong. My intuition has been honed over the past few months, and I have learned to listen to her.

I push the key that Kevin gave me into the lock. I quietly guide the door open while slipping the key in my pocket and pulling out my pistol. I enter the room.

My knife points my way through the dark while I grip my pistol in my other hand. I approach the sleeping leader. I don't even know what to call him, don't even know his name or rank. Playing over in my mind is another calculation: should I let him live? Work out a truce? Or should I enact the original plan?

I stand next to his bed. His knee is upright, and he is covered in a draped blanket cast in the moonlight coming through the window, almost like a statue on a sarcophagus. He is not moving.

He is too still, like he is not even breathing. I wonder if he is already dead, but I realize with utter fear that he is holding his breath. Maybe he smells me. Maybe he senses me in the room. Maybe his intuition is finely honed too.

Under the blanket, his arm starts to slowly move toward something.

"Do not do it," I whisper.

He stops, probably confused by the soft, girly voice ordering him to halt. He turns toward me. His face is chiseled — big jaw, hard nose. Deep-set eyes blink a couple of times, trying to take me in, my bright eyes set into the darkened room and dark skin, laureled below a halo of leaves.

"Ah, so you're the little nigger bitch," he finally says in a voice deep and rough.

"I thought you were a myth, a lie my men made up to blame rivalry killings on."

"Nope. I put your men down."

"I didn't believe it. No way some dirty black devil-girl was killing my men. But I still put a bounty on you. Made it seem like I cared. Two girls for you dead, three girls for you alive."

I do not know what to make of this at first: girls for me dead or alive? But then I understand. Now my calculation is tallied. I will not be making peace tonight.

"Still raping and enslaving, I see. Well, thank you, I guess. You are making this very easy for me."

I place the tip of my knife on his chest, above his heart, to freeze him still. He takes in a shallow, desperate breath to avoid the knife point. But as the knife hovers above him, he laughs a weak but sinister laugh. His levity in the face of death throws me off.

"Like you're much better," he says.

I watch for his arms under the blanket, expecting that he is just trying to distract me with his mouth, so he can attack me with his hands. Against my intuition or maybe because of it, I look back at his eyes and let him finish.

"Oh, you don't know, do you? How precious."

"What?"

9

"You don't know why Pax killed Kevin."

Kevin is dead! What? Our hero, our leader is actually gone?

This does it. I am distracted. Before he can use his words against me, my instinct pounces. I jump onto the bed and straddle his body. I press his arms together with my knees. Between my weight and the tangled blanket, he cannot move. I place the knife blade against his throat to guarantee it.

Now that he is pinned, I can think. I knew that my chances of finding Kevin and Pax after they stomped off into the forest on some stupid male challenge were slim, were narrowing as the weeks passed, but I did not know Kevin was dead and that Pax killed him.

"Why?" I ask.

He laughs again, a sick, twisted giggle that sounds odd coming from such a muscular body. He probably knows he is going to die and is sowing the last bit of evil he can in the world, one last desperate attack against our tribe. I must weigh this against whatever will come out of his mouth next.

"Pax killed Kevin because he sold girls into sexual slavery."

The idea is so preposterous I am ready to end him now, but hairs stand up on the back of my neck.

"What girls?" I ask, but my voice is weak. My intuitive calculations seem to already know the answer, a sinking feeling in my gut.

"You know," he says. "The teenage girls from the other barracks. The ones you never saw again, dead or alive, after you killed our countrymen—eh, my countrymen. And that's not even the worst of it. After he traded those girls for sheep, he let the militia into the base. So the other girls left behind, the ones I saved from the terrorists and offered up to my men for your bounty, they're grateful; they're even willing, because I saved them from a much worse fate."

"How do you know this?" I ask.

"Kevin. He called us on the radio and mocked us right after you all killed our compatriots. He confessed his crimes and challenged us to come up and stop him, taunted us with: 'All you can ever do is play counting coup with death. Come play with death,' he said."

He laughs again, his coarse, mocking laugh to turn the screws of his final insult now that he is facing death, playing with death, at my hands.

"You know, I was going to let you live," I say. "I was going to propose a peace. A truce: your soldiers stay on your side of the river, and our tribe stays on ours. If your troops kept the peace, I would stop hunting them down. But since you told me what you told me, I just decided to go with Plan A, Kevin's plan. He always thought three moves ahead. That's probably why he taunted you. Got you to attack the militia for him. But he also kept a key to the major's room knowing we might need it to sneak back in one day."

He thinks about this for a while. It looks like he is contemplating his chances of survival if he begs for his life by accepting peace. He looks into my eyes to try to read me.

"If you kill me, they're still going to come after your tribe. They're never going to stop. The fear and vulnerability will make them even more fierce. You and your friends will never be safe. I am your only chance at peace."

"Do you know what fracking is?" I ask. He narrows his eyes. "I am going to frack you. Your men, the ones that you assume are killing each other, the ones that rival for your spot and the *spoils* you can offer as bounty, they will think your death is an inside job, and they will pick each other apart competing for the throne." I move my face close to his, but keep my blade steady on his throat. He knows this is true. "You see, within a group the selfish individual always wins, but between groups...between groups, the selfless group always wins. I learned that in my biology class!"

Before he can respond or yell out, I pull my face and knife back, then hit him hard across the jaw with the butt of the pistol in my other hand.

He is out cold, but just to make sure, I bring the pistol handle down hard on his head again. I hop off the bed and put the knife and pistol away. I am eager to finish the job and get out of this evil room and off the decadent base.

I clutch two grenades in my hand like rare, forbidden fruit, then place them on the bed and unravel two already measured pieces of cord and tie around the pins of each grenade. I tuck them tight under his arm, against his body, and string the cord along as I back my way out of the room. I pause at the door, slowly open it, and look down the long, empty hallway.

I move into the hallway and close the door above the unreeling cord. The strings are fully unraveled when I toss them through the window. I follow them with a quick hop to the other side. I compose myself on the ledge and turn around. I close the window, only leaving an inch open for the strings to pass through.

A deep breath flows in and out as I prepare for the final race from the base. In my mind, I play the route over and over, and start believing that I can make it before anyone notices me after the explosions.

I pull hard on the cords and take off in a careful dash along the ledge. I reel the cords around my hand as I run to the edge of the building, jumping back to the low-level roof. The grenade pins ding against the window and chase me along the roof. I jump to the ground, and they bounce off my back as I take off in my full, fast sprint toward the fence. The pins are now fully reeled in and gripped in my fist.

The eminent explosions drive my furious pace. It happens.

Kaboom! Kaboom!

The building shakes, but I am already near the fence. I crouch down and slide through the hole. Dirt embeds into my fingernails as I keep my body down and frantically crawl through the tall grass. I want to reach the safety of the forest before I am seen. If I am spotted, then this plan and this kill was a waste.

My canine crawl, it turns out, is almost as spooky fast as my upright run, kicking up dirt and splitting the tall grass that snaps off my face. I reach the forest, right back to the cord-marked tree without having to look for it. I find my costume and slide underneath her, like wrapping myself in a security blanket or a mother's love. I cuddle up against my rifle and allow myself a look back at the base.

The scope is out and pressed against my eye. I scan the room I just escaped. The window is blown out, and smoke from the grenades snake up and out into the night air. Rays from flashlights slice back and forth through the haze. I see my crows circling around the blasted room. They glide through the smoke and light, hoping I left them some scraps.

I continue to wait, making sure the light stays in the blown-out room. I am scared that tiki torches will ablaze and line up in a posse streaking out toward the forest to hunt for me. Instead, the foreboding beams stay contained and are punctuated by loud shouts and, finally, gunshots. I am safe. Our planned worked.

But now I must wrestle with what I saw and the things he said. His devil tongue may have laid the seeds of evil. And that *figure-Y* will haunt me for not knowing who that person was or why they were tortured and killed, another mystery I must solve. And I must suffer the reality that my true grand quarry, the search for Kevin, might have been a waste of time.

I gather my gear and head back into the forest. Behind me, I can hear the squawks of my crows, angry that I left nothing for them to feast on.

6
___

NORMAL

(Michael)

Normalcy is a threadbare blanket, or better yet, a mother's teat. Held firm in her embrace, we are kept warm and fed. No matter what rages beyond her grasp, we have the feeling of security and safety. But we are only as safe as the mother holding us.

The tribe keeps busy in normalcy, blind to the evil beyond our valley and our village of Caxm, too nervous and too fragile to dwell on what is going on in a post-coup America or anywhere else. We are isolated and have heard nothing, and by focusing on tasks, they think they are safe.

From my Humvee, I watch people work, embraced in the warmth of routine. The yurts are finished. Charlotte connected the pounded felt together with thick thread made from the sinew and skin of slaughtered sheep. Jaden's designs decorate the walls, pictures of doors, stars, and mountains, colored in gray and black ash from the campfire and reddish clay that looks more like dried blood as the days pass.

Still, the yurts are personal, theirs. Habitats for their habits. Ten yurts in total with about eight or nine people sharing each domicile. The nights are getting colder, but they have each other to keep warm. I sleep alone, but I still light two candles commemorating Hector and Sam's deaths to offer slight comfort. Every morning, about the time the candles burn down, I wake from the backseat of my Humvee and watch people emerge from the yurts.

They lift the flaps and flitter out with a fake dreariness of facing another day of work. They stretch their arms up high and yawn. They lumber over to the campfire for breakfast, then head out to take on the tasks for the day or for morning prayers.

Spencer leads the LDS, and others who have joined, in prayers. They go to a yurt especially designed for them. After their morning devotions, they exit and head to the large gardens to toil.

They silently walk by the original villagers, old Muslims who point their prayer rugs and genuflections west toward Mecca. West, back toward the road from which we drove the Humvees in months before. They, too, are now joined by other members of our tribe. Normalcy, it seems, isn't the only threadbare blanket to cling to in a storm.

Jaden and Seth hurry around with the monumental task of construction. With each thrust of the shovel or beat of the hammer, they attempt to knock the looks of suffering away from their faces. With a few others, they cut lumber and architect designs. They build yurts, sheds, irrigations canals to the new fields we have sown. They keep busy constructing and building so they don't have to focus on the destruction that brought us here. The battles that left Seth's twin brother, Sam, for whom this village is named, dead and buried in a hole by the river.

The battles that left Jaden burned, wounded, and gun-shy. Jaden and I were good friends, and I can't remember the last time we have talked. Sadder, still, I can't remember us sharing a smile since the flagpole.

Felicia isn't pushing away the past. She watches the road often while carrying a rifle and at the same time, her baby, Hector Jr., snuggled tight in a wrap against her body. Her face is always stern and ready for battle. She gets plenty of help from the older villagers and her friends, but she always keeps her rifle and baby close. She remembers what took Hector Sr. away from her, and she, more than anyone here, has the most to lose and the most to fear. Felicia knows Hector Jr. is only as safe as the mother holding him.

Everyone else keeps busy to push those traumas further into the past. Everyone except Felicia, Fetty, and me. Fetien comes in every few days to resupply. She is working. She contributes. Animals she has hunted in the forest are a key staple in our soup. Her hunting gives us variety and prevents the need to kill too many sheep, but her work is not a distraction. Her face doesn't show the fake concern around tasks to accomplish. No, her face carries a different weight, pulled down heavy by more tribulations every time she enters our village. Fetty, in her odd costume, followed by her bizarre band of corvids. Everyone else doesn't notice the strange murder of crows that only appear when Fetty does. The birds are larger than the ones in America, black still, but touched with a gray crest the color of ash.

Fetty is hunting. I am not sure for what, but she carries the weight of the world on her shoulders. And she looks at the tribe in the same manner I do—like an outsider.

Annie and Paco disappear for days at a time, too, taking their herd of sheep further from the village of Caxm. Sheep dogs always bounce around them and welcome the village eagerly every time they return, always cause for a celebration, a holiday from mundane tasks. Annie and Paco are in love with each other and the liberty they have found in the hills. The happy sheep dogs and the allure of making love under the stars, away from the crowded yurts, brings their own celebrants, other polyamorous lovers who worship freedom like a religion and join Annie and Paco's flock for mini-vacations away from their daily tasks and routineness. I can't begrudge them their happiness.

Eva and Cisco oversee the other herd of sheep, and us. They keep the flock close to the village. Eva rides horseback and prances around like she is in charge. She even has a cowboy hat to boot. I am not sure where she got it, or the horses for that matter. She also keeps her rifle close, always on guard. She stays near the tribe and barks orders from the saddle like she is sitting on a throne. She throws my idleness an occasional harsh glance, but she knows better than to boss me around; I know the secret that lead us into the tenuous safety of the valley, the terrible crime we are both guilty of abetting, and pressing me would expose that shadowplay.

Lupina leads, too, but in her subtle way. She goes around and checks on everyone, including me. She is the only one from the old tribe who doesn't ignore me, but still, her interactions are just a kind smile, a weak wave, and the occasional knock on the window followed by the obligatory, "You OK?"

Like Fetty, she wears worry on her face. When she checks on me, I answer only with a nod. I don't ask how she is doing. No one here is OK. Lupina lost her love when Pax stomped off into the forest with Kevin, and not knowing his fate is worse than digging another hole and lighting another candle. Conversing with Lupina about how we all are doing would unearth the fact that we are all wondering what happened to Pax and Kevin, our best friends.

No one else from the Tribe of Iodine Wine interacts with me. Kevin and Pax are gone. Jaden is too beaten down, and maybe he and the others feel guilty that they couldn't save me from being chained and whipped at the flagpole. Even Charlotte, who did the unspeakable to save my life, killed a guard at the gate to start the Battle of the Base, keeps her glances to a minimum. I must remind her of what she had to do and what we've all become.

My only true, pure interaction is with one of the old ladies from the original village we all share now, locals and our tribe. Anahita brings me food: mutton wrapped in flatbread with curious sauces and herbs. Oh, and sweet nougats, dried fruit, and nuts, which I admit taste wonderful. She has taken to sitting with me in the Humvee lately, basking in my strong silence and the greenhouse heat. She must find sanctuary being near the biggest man with the biggest guns. Sometimes she even sings, a quiet, wispy song that she chants over and over.

Anahita's hazel eyes are nuzzled beneath ancient wrinkles and take on the purple hues of her hijab. Eyes and withered skin as soft as her calm melody which warms me as she sings the verses with such tranquility. The song nearly makes me forget the horrors of the past with a soft voice that can almost make me feel safe.

BUT WE ARE ONLY as safe as the mother holding us, and this grandmother who sings to me is not safe, and neither are we. Worse, she is in more danger now that we are here.

So, instead of sucking off the teat of normalcy and false safety, I sit in the Humvee and think a lot about the world, about our bloody past, and about what lies ahead of us. I think about what Kevin said before he slipped through the fence and escaped from the base. America had just broken out into civil war, and Kevin knew what was coming next. Even halfway around the world in Tajikistan, he knew the chaos would come for us.

Kevin said, "If America falls, the world falls. What comes next — the brutality, oppression, savagery — that's the norm; that's the bulk of human history. We just kept it at bay. And when it comes, it will come for us with a vengeance."

Brutality, oppression, savagery. That's the norm, not this façade of busyness and work.

I remember once, back in high school—and *damn*, that was less than a year ago—I was in AP world history. The teacher had a habit of ignoring me. The presence of a big, six-foot-four, biracial kid elicits a host of reactions: fear, fake niceness, sportsy camaraderie, unearned brotherhood. But usually, I just get sideways, dismissive glances. The teacher was of that ilk. The only time he talked to me was at the beginning of the year when he asked me, three times, if I was in the right class. Even made a joke about my size, the old, petrified coot assuming I should be in a strength and conditioning class and not AP history. All his esteemed knowledge and not knowing I won my middle school geography bee three years in a row, not knowing that I already scored a perfect five on AP geography the year before, not knowing that I had the maps of Africa and Europe memorized, countries and capitals. He had a picture of progress, and my nappy hair, dark skin, and big body were not part of it.

The teacher lived in the past and loved, *just loved*, the study of civilization. His walls were decorated by the portraits of so many esteemed white men. From Marcus Aurelius to Shakespeare, from Hemingway to Hegel, he believed in the progress of history like it was scripture. And he preached from the pulpit about how we were building a better world, fulfilling our destiny from the stone age to the space age.

Then, over Christmas break, we were given a homework assignment to make a timeline of history. I remember seeing and studying these in the hallways the year before. Butcher paper streaming long lines of civilization's advancement, punctuated with pictures of art and quotes from literature and historical figures, all a testament to amazing accomplishments.

Fed up with his worship of progress and the chorus of coots surrounding the room, I decided to make my own, special timeline for the project. I titled my project the Red Wave. With Kevin's help, we researched and documented people brutally killed by civilization. Instead of works of art or esteemed accomplishments, we highlighted atrocities like the conquests of Genghis Kahn, the Mideast and Atlantic Slave Trade, countless rebellions in China, the Wars of Religion, and advent of Communism. We even added trendlines for the crazy high rates of murder, infanticide, and rape that were just the norm "back in the day."

At Kevin's house, we spread out the butcher map on the long dining room table. Mark, Kevin's dad, got into the project, too. He helped with the research, recommending different color swim lanes for different parts of the world. But across the timeline, we marked out the red stars totaling the number of people killed each decade, tallying up the dead across each color-coded civilization.

We connected the stars across the decades with lines drawn in blood red markers, spiking the constant flow of atrocities like continuous waves. My butcher paper of butchering cascaded with the 20th Century Hemoclysm: the pinnacle of connected bloodshed crossing two world wars and multiple totalitarian regimes that killed over two hundred million people. Two hundred million people. Killed.

Roll tide.

And then it dropped. The rates of deaths and destruction declined toward the end of the last century with the absence of total wars between major powers and the sanctity of international law and freedom. Despite the constant barrage by fear-mongering media, we were actually living in the safest time in human history. But the long, crimson wave didn't disappear, it only ebbed back for a bit, like a drained beach before a tsunami crashes. The peace hit a pause, a several-decade vacation from the bloodlettings. For white people, maybe a bit longer of a break. For black people, maybe a bit shorter or not at all. Kevin was right; America just kept the savagery at bay, but a hole in the earth opened-up and brought it back. The explosion released the toxicity through a terrorist attack, as the government claimed. Or through a government ploy, as Kevin once secretly told me.

And the tribe is blind to the reemerging chaos as they shuffle through the tasks of the day, clinging to the teat of busyness.

No, my teats are the .50 calibers sitting above me. I nestle beneath their warm bosom. My routine is cleaning each one every other day. Doing pushups, squats, curls, lifting rocket boxes of ammunition over and over to keep my arms strong for the big guns. I am never more than a few feet from the trucks. I charge up the batteries once a week. I maintain the weapons and vehicles to make sure everything is ready for the day when the warm blanket of work and normalcy is pulled away from us, and we are left naked and bare, again, to what the world has always really been. The last time that happened, I was tortured while chained to a flagpole. I will stay near the .50 calibers for when that vengeance comes again.

Because the normalcy my tribe clings to — that of labor and tasks, morning stretches and hot tea — is the routine from their old world. They are holding on to a past that has evaporated, absorbed back into our brutal history which reemerged when a hole in the ground blew ash into the air. They think we are safe here in this valley, tucked under fruit trees and huddled in hand-made yurts. Because I can feel the venomousness in the air. I can sense the reborn disorder and death collecting around us again. And that explosion wasn't a cataclysm that brought on the apocalypse. Nope. Not even close.

I feel the truth straight through to my bones. This isn't the start of the apocalypse. No, this is just the return to our normal. The Red Wave is back.

And I am ready for it.

7

THE WEB

(Fetien)

I am safe, but I pick up my running pace. I set a dangerous stride through the trees away from the base and destruction I just caused. My mind is swirling. The weight of what the fracked leader said, of what I have always known, deep down, to be true, is pushing me forward like momentum and gravity down a mountain. Kevin sold the girls—Brittany, Lily, and Kelly—into sexual slavery. And Pax killed him for it.

I always thought of Pax as such a pompous ass. With his blind entitlements, he bumbled his way into conversations, into opinions, into leadership positions with alarming ignorance. His jealousy of Kevin's raw talents and allure. His male gaze. But for all his faults, Pax is not—was not?—a killer. His innocence was part of what made him so naïve and unaware. What could push him to kill his best friend? Was it jealousy of Kevin's position as our leader and savior? Did he hold empathy for the girls peddled to a terrible fate? Or did he think he was protecting the tribe, and especially Lupina, from Kevin and his machinations?

And Kevin—his pessimistic worldliness that attracted me—the brooding eyes and killer sensitivities. Being so sensitive to people is a double-edged sword. You also sense their weaknesses and know best how to hurt them.

That gloom, that ability to see weakness and win, makes him capable of terrible things. What he said, before the fifty-mile trek, when we talked in the heat: "And they will meet my darkness." Even though we were both placed in leadership positions by the military, he was already orchestrating his revenge, his coup. Knowing Kevin, he probably started planning the use of the girls as pawns the moment they threatened him on the plane. We saw aggressive, popular girls throwing temper tantrums for not getting their way, but he saw an opportunity, a three-move plan to use their attractiveness against them.

I break through branches and bramble and stop when I reach a clearing. When? When did this happen? I stop and stare at the rising sun breaking over mountains and trees.

Where did they go? When did the crime happen? When did they trade the girls?

I need to map this out; to make sure, I must make a timeline with all the events. For all I know, the leader I just killed spun a wicked web of lies to cause turmoil within our group in the same way my fracking of him did to his tribe. I don't have any empirical proof, but I can run events through logical and temporal tests.

I head to my nest, a rocky outcropping about two miles away. My run is slow and even, but I am eager to get there. My home away from home on the dark side of the river where I can think and figure out this problem. I have supplies and food there. I need to rest and reason out a timeline of this crime.

The nest is safe due to the hidden vantage points looking down on all approaches. The rocks offer shelter and shield against attack. They sit on a hillock surrounded by trees that allow my crows to perch and spot anyone coming from a distance.

I reach the nest in short time, and my crows are already waiting for me. A few weeks back, they alerted me to an attack. They took off from their perches and squawked their loud ka-kaws. From deep inside the nest's shadows I watched the floating birds above a group of four soldiers slowly crawling toward my hideout. They were covered in camouflage and hard to spot, but my crows saw them right way.

I snuck out the backside of my nest and double-backed down the hill and all the way around the squad of soldiers coming my way. Following their trail was easy. I just needed to look up to the sky. As they slowly stalked toward my nest, I got up close. I took them all out before they could even turn around.

My crows ate well for a week. They even invited their wolf friends to the feast. I watched them do it. A few crows flew off and a short while later cautious wolves followed their return. They snuck through the forest and approached the dead men.

Seems I am not only one with a symbiotic relationship with the crows. The *steppenwolves* cracked open the bounty, tearing at the clothes and flesh so the crows could pick at more than just eyeballs and tongues. I sat on one of the boulders, like a royal on a twisted throne — the queen of badlands and carrion—watching the wolves and crows consume my enemies.

When they finished their feast, I went down to scavenge. I removed the guns and supplies from the bloody heap of bones and fabric. I carried my bounty back up to my nest, adding it to my collection, a pile, cuddled against a boulder and covered with a thin tarp. I could arm my own platoon, if I only had friends beyond the crows and wolves.

So, I am safe in the nest surrounded by loyal scavengers and the picked bones of those who tried to kill me, those who tracked me down, whose ultimate goal was to wipe out my tribe. But my mind is spinning. The world has gone upside down, again. I had no trouble killing before because it kept us safe. Kept us away from the type of men who tried to rape me and whipped Michael for stopping the brutal attack. The type of men who killed the professional soldiers in the middle of the night through exhaust fed into their barracks.

"These men deserved to die, and the world is better for it." I kept telling myself that as I pulled the trigger over and over. But now. Now!?

"Like you're much better," the leader said before I fracked him.

Are we? Are we much better? Did we sell girls into sexual slavery? Into a lifetime of rape and brutality? And did Kevin orchestrate this?

My emotions need to be removed from this equation. I must solve this problem without the influence of what was done to me and what I have done. Be scientific. Be objective.

I glide past the tall boulders and take off my costume, leaving her propped against a boulder next to my rifle.

The cords made an X across my body unravel as I spool them away from my torso. I tie one end to a crag in a rock and spin like a ballerina across my nest. Unwound, I attach the thick twine tight to a small tree on the other side.

I take thinner pieces of cord and cut them into small strips. I lay the pieces in similar colored piles on a flat boulder that serves as my dining room table. I look down at the cords, green, black, red, and yellow. I stare at the multi-colored piles and think about the principle people involved.

"Kevin," I mutter to myself. I pick up the black cords and put them in my left front pocket.

I place the green cords into my right pocket. "Pax," I say.

I stare at the remaining two colors. I do not want to say his name. I do not want to give a voice to the dark thought creeping in my mind. My hero. The one who saved me could also be the villain. I shut my eyes and say, "Michael." I pick up the red cords and put them in my back, left pocket.

I shake my head in disdain. "And you, Eva. How could you?

You always had a coldness to you and a crazy crush on Kevin, but this. This?" I put the yellow cords in my back, right pocket.

"No pre-judgements," I tell myself. "Figure this out first."

I turn around and head back to the start of the thick line strung across my nest. I wish for paper and pen to write this out, but I have neither.

"When did it all begin?" I ask the crows. "When Kevin left," I respond for them. I take a black cord and tie it to the beginning of the line. I knot it twice as a symbol for *gone from the tribe*. Kevin left us when he found out about the civil war breaking out back home. He knew it would spread to our base, so he escaped to the forest. I wanted to follow him but stayed behind. I was too scared and too hesitant to chase after him into the dark.

What happened after Kevin left? Well, nothing, for a while. It was boring, a calm before the storm. I snuck out of the base early one morning and ran through the forest looking for Kevin, but never found him. Why did I never find him? Where did he go? He was communicating with Michael and Annie, so he was close. Did he want to avoid me? I will get back to this later.

Then the storm. I came back from an early morning run to see Annie and Pax building an obstacle course. I helped them make a pyramid of old tires and everyone, even kids from the other barracks, came and helped build the course. Wait, no—Michael, Eva, Jaden, and some other black kids refused to help because one of the boys from the other barracks called Jaden the n-word.

Anyway, we built the obstacle course, and had a competition between all the barracks. Pax, Sam, oh, poor Sam, me, Paco, and Annie were the runners for our tribe. We were winning, but Annie never finished the last round because one of the kids from the other barracks cheated and knocked her off the pyramid. She broke her elbow, and Paco went on a rampage. He beat up a handful of kids from the other barracks and was pummeling the cheater when Lupina yelled at him to stop.

Then what happened? We returned to our barracks. Lupina wrapped Annie's arm then got in an argument with Charlotte.

Charlotte was pissed that we were mixing with the other kids after what they called Jaden.

Hairs start to stand up on my back. Then Pax and Lupina left. Where did they go? We were drinking alcohol the other barracks made, and Lupina went to go check on the kid Paco beat up, but they never returned that night, at least not while I was awake.

I tie a green cord on the line a few lengths right of Kevin's black cord. Pax and Lupina never came back that night and the next morning...the next morning the storm starts. The racist corporal stormed into our barracks firing his gun into the ceiling, and the soldiers grabbed Paco. We were forced to meet for an assembly, and Paco was exiled over the fence.

We soon learned that the National Guard soldiers, the ones tasked with keeping order at the base while the professional soldiers fought on the outside, these Guards, these cowards, killed the professional soldiers with exhaust the night before, as an extension of the civil war.

The night the soldiers were murdered Pax and Lupina disappeared. How did the new leader, who I just killed, know Pax killed Kevin? Was Pax conspiring with the National Guard? I cannot see him, or especially Lupina, doing such a thing, but I must consider this scenario.

I take another green cord and tie it in an open "O" around the rope. Where did Pax go the night of the exhaust? Is he a traitor?

OK. I must think clearly. This next part is hard. After the National Guard took over, they made us slaves. No other way to put it. They forced us at gunpoint to bury the bodies of the professional soldiers they murdered. I helped carry the major's body out to the big hole in the earth we had dug earlier.

And then...the next day. We were building latrines. "Do I need to revisit this? Yes. Do not be emotional," I tell myself.

I do not need to mark my absence on the line. I know where I was and who I am. I am Fetien Mihirät. And I am a survivor.

. . .

THE NEXT DAY five men with guns tried to gang rape me. And Michael saved me. They pinned me to the ground then Michael attacked them. Weaponless, he knocked out a couple of soldiers and freed me. I ran to the fence and escaped out of the same hole Kevin snuck through. I looked back to see Michael, unconscious, on the ground. The soldiers were standing around him, nursing their wounds, but looking down at him like my crows look at a felled prey.

I take a deep breath and close my eyes. I was safe, but Michael was not. I escaped into to the forest while Michael was chained to the flagpole.

I open my eyes and pull out a red cord for Michael. "What happened to you on the flagpole, Michael?" I ask the red line. I heard via Kevin and later stories that Michael was whipped in front of everyone. This public punishment is what convinced the tribe to fight back. Later that night we attacked the base. Wait. Slow down. This is important.

Charlotte dressed up like a prostitute to kill the guard at the gate. I could hardly recognize her when we met her in the guard-house, after she slit his throat. Then we ran to Michael and freed him. Kevin cut his chains, and we split up.

Why did we split up? Because of the guns. We were short on guns, only Kevin and Paco had rifles. Wait. Where did they get their weapons? This seems important. Save for later. I too was given a weapon, but it was the guard's that Charlotte killed. Since I had a gun, I met up with and led the kids from our barracks who chose to fight. My group consisted of my classmates from East High School and the Utah kids. Pax was in my group.

Paco led the other group. He and his Mexican friends stormed into the National Guard's barracks, while I took my group to the motor pool.

I start to feel a strong sensation in the pit of my stomach. Kevin took Eva and Michael to the officer's quarters. Why did he take them? And why the officer's quarters? This is where the evil corporal slept. The one who whipped Michael. I thought, at the time, that Kevin just wanted to be the one to kill the king and wanted Michael to get his revenge. But why Eva too? And not only did the corporal and his cronies sleep there, but so did the girls from the other barracks, Lily, Becky, and Kelly. They were sleeping with the corporal and his cronies for a privileged position.

I reluctantly take out a black, red, and yellow cord from my pockets and snake them together. I tie the intertwined cords to the line. Damn. If they went into the officer's quarters, they were the last ones to be with the girls.

Hold on. Back to the battle. I shot the guards at the motor pool. Danny picked up one of their rifles, and Jaden picked up the other. We were in the motor pool getting two Humvees started when other soldiers attacked us. We were pinned down but firing back when they threw a grenade into the building. Jaden was hurt and down. Pax picked up his weapon, but we were outgunned, and I was worried about our chances when more firing lit up outside. Then Michael and Kevin came into the motor pool. They snuck up on the soldiers shooting at us and took them out from behind. After that, Kevin gave a quick demo on the fifty calibers to Danny and Michael. They manned the big machine-guns while Sam and Seth drove them out of the building. With the big guns, we had no trouble taking out the rest of the guards.

Wait a minute. Michael and Kevin saved us at the motor pool, but where was Eva? She was with them when they attacked the officers' quarters but never joined us.

And where did Pax go? Was he with Jaden in the motor pool? I am sure he came with us to continue the attack. He had one of the rifles, and because I was leading the group, I was tracking who had guns and who did not. Then he disappeared after the fighting died down. I take another green cord for Pax, and a yellow one for Eva, and wrap long the line.

After the battle was over, Paco and Felicia rushed out of the barracks carrying Hector. Poor Hector. We loaded him and Jaden into a truck rushed him to Lupina for medical attention, but Hector died.

The next day we buried Hector after we burned the dead National Guard soldiers in a big, horrendous funeral pyre. That day, the toxic black smoke was scorched into my brain. I visualize the scene, all of us standing around Hector's grave, the smell of the burning soldiers, the sad words and crying for Hector. It is something I will never forget. And I am now sure of a startling fact: Eva was absent.

I tie another yellow cord to the line. Pax was there. He came back from wherever he went after the battle, but Eva never showed up again until a few days later. No, wait. She was at the meeting Kevin called. I remember her saying something about the book, *Lord of the Flies*. Yesenia was commenting how our situation was like the movie, and she wished the soldiers would come and save us already, then Eva rudely told her it was a book before it was a movie.

Then Kevin said, "The soldiers were coming, they just weren't coming to save us." This seems important. Did Kevin know an attack was imminent from the other base? Yes, he knew because he called the other base on the radio and taunted them, daring them to attack us.

After the meeting, Kevin directed Felicia and Spencer to make peace with the other teenagers hiding in their barracks. Then... then, Kevin left with Eva and Michael on his mission. They were gone for three days while we prepared for the exodus into the mountains. When they returned Kevin was shepherding the sheep.

We soon headed on a trek into the mountains. On the first night at camp, Pax disappeared again. I know this because Lupina was looking for him in the morning. I place another green string further down the line. Then he reemerged when the four Humvees attacked us, and Sam was killed. Did Pax go to the enemy and tell them where we were? He came out of the forest near the soldiers attacking us.

After we beat the soldiers back, we hustled the tribe to a bridge. I hung back looking for followers but crossed the bridge right before Kevin burnt it to keep us from being chased.

On the other side of the river, Pax seemed to be acting weird. By the time we got to the next camp he yelled some odd things at Kevin. He did say something about *the girls.* And he said something about boys he killed, during the attack by the Humvees. What did that mean? As soon as he said it, Kevin challenged him to prove he killed the boys. And they disappeared into the forest and have not returned. I snake green and black cords together and bookend the timeline.

OK. I need to string this all together. Ha.

Problem one: Pax may be a traitor. He may have sold us out to the bad people in charge. Evidence for this: First, Lupina and he disappeared on the night the National Guard killed the professional soldiers. Second, Pax has always been jealous of Kevin. Third, Pax disappeared again the night the enemy found us on the road. Forth, the leader I just blew up said Pax killed Kevin, and he knew why. How would he know this unless he was communicating with Pax? Unless...unless he tortured Pax for the information. I think of the *figure-Y,* the crucified man I just saw near the flagpole and shudder. He was too tall to be Kevin, but the right height for Pax.

Do not get emotional.

Evidence against Pax being a traitor: Lupina would never be part of it. She is too honest and kind. Unless she was just trying to make peace in her foolish way...hmmm...still seems unlikely. Also, Pax was part of the battle against the National Guard. But he never fired his weapon and disappeared in the middle of it.

Problem two: Kevin, Michael, and Eva sold the girls into sexual slavery.

Evidence for this: First, I never saw the girls, dead or alive, after the battle. Second, Kevin had guns before the battle and sheep after their mission. How could he get both for free? Third, the leader, though under duress, said that Kevin sold girls into slavery. And he said Kevin let the militia into the base after. Is that why we were in such a hurry to leave? Is that why the base looked more damaged than when we left? Fourth, Michael, Kevin, and

Eva attacked the officer's quarters where the girls were sleeping. Michael and Kevin joined us in the battle after, but without Eva. Was she guarding the girls? But how did she come back for the meeting? And who was guarding the girls then? Is there another guilty person?

Evidence against: First, Eva, Michael, and Kevin were together, away from the possible kidnapped girls for the meeting Kevin called. But could someone else have been guarding them? If so, who? Second, the leader tonight could be lying, causing disruption in our group, the same way I caused destruction in his. But this seems like a very intricate lie to come up with in the middle of the night after being woken and surprised with a knife against your throat. Third, Michael would never do this. He saved me from being raped. How could he then allow others to be raped? Michael...Michael, what happened to you before the Battle of the Base? He was never the same after that night. Maybe the flagpole changed him into a man who could do such a thing.

Michael is the key. And there is only one way to find out for sure.

8

ACTUALLY

(Michael)

∿

We wake to something familiar but scary. I am watching from my usual spot in the Humvee when I see white flakes float through the air. At first, I thought it was more ash, sparse now, only appearing when a hard wind brings a fresh dusting.

But we realize as we start our morning chores that it's not ash, but snow. Everyone stops working to look up at the sky, at the small flakes slowly falling. They reach out their hands as if receiving alms. They hold out their tongues to catch the snowflakes.

Being from Colorado and Utah, we are all used to piles and piles of snow. The first snow of the season comes with elation. Snow means snowboarding and skiing, snowball fights, Christmas, and *Walking in a Winter Wonderland*.

I watch the tribe react to this first snow as if they are still children back in our nice neighborhoods, eager to head to the sledding hill at City Park. They laugh and spin and dance with the falling flakes, but slowly, their joy fades with the descending flurry. Snow, here, means a coming cold, heavy with unknowns. Will we have enough food to survive the winter? Did Charlotte and the others make and mend enough clothes? What are winters like in the mountains? And what kind of winter will the ash bring?

As the flurries increase in intensity, everyone stops playing and gets back to work. Back to the control of the known, keen now to get more done before the ominous winter sweeps over us.

EARLIER THAN USUAL, Anahita joins me in the Humvee. She brings a pot of hot tea and nuts with day-old flat bread to share. The tea smells fruity and earthy and is scalding hot to protect against the new coldness surrounding us. Anahita seems nervous. Her hands shake as she pours the tea. Maybe she is worried about the approaching change of seasons. Maybe she knows how much food and clothing we will need and knows we are short.

She hands me a cup of tea then puts the pot down on the floorboard, picks up her mug, lifting it with weathered hands to pursed lips. A thin stream exhales through pursed lips into the mug as steam rises and frolics around her hooked nose and closed eyes. She rocks back and forth then releases a soft, harmonizing hum.

She starts the song again. The melody she has chanted to me over and over. With eyes shut and tea clutched like an oracle, the familiar song seems to take on extra poignancy. I see a tiny tear sneak out through her wrinkles as she sings:

"Dastamro Ba dast gired
   Vaqte ki şumo tarsed
   Va agar duo gūjam, agar az on ço Berun şaved
   Ba ū tasallī joBed, Ba ū kūmak kuned
   Fahmed, ki jagon varaqi şinovar nest
   NovoBasta az on,

Va heç sir
NovoBasta az on, ki cī guna Badraftorī
Metavoned sadoi xudro zahrolud kuned
Jo turo az şodī nigoh dor"

SHE FINISHES the song and moves her hand from the mug to cover my fist. It is soft with age and warm from the tea. She opens her eyes and looks at me with a deep, wise gaze. She seems to be struggling with what to say, and I wish I had spent more of my idle time learning her Tajiki language.

"Winter, years past," she starts in broken English. "Civil war here, too."

This is why she was laboring so much to talk, why she is so nervous — she is going to talk to me in the English she has been learning from our tribe. She takes a long pause and struggles with the next statement.

"They came for my daughters." She stops and closes her eyes.

Why is she telling me this? What does she know?

"They came for my daughters," she repeats then shakes her head. She can't continue in any language. Their civil war occurred decades ago, after the fall of the Soviet Union, but she cannot relive it. She only pats my hand and opens her eyes, set beneath a well of tears.

"You find peace," she tells me. In any language, I can tell she is lying, but I love her for trying.

We sit still. Holding hands, sipping tea, watching the snowflakes fall. She starts humming her song again. I look back to her and wonder what pain and suffering she has seen in her long lifetime. Cynically, I wonder if it was worth living.

"You find peace," I repeat. A smile breaks through her humming lips.

I smile, too.

"Find peace." Anahita points outside. I follow her crooked finger to the foggy and snow-speckled windshield. I can make out the sharp lines of a rifle just beyond the gauze. I take my hand and wipe the fog away from the glass. Fetty is holding the rifle. She stands on the hood of the Humvee staring at me with her piercing gaze, bristling with the branches and leaves of her camouflage. Above, Fetty's murder of crows circle, forming a halo around her in the falling snow. They swoop in and out of clear view between fogged and cleaned glass. She steps closer to the glass and bends over to look right at me.

"Michael!" she yells.

SINCE FRESHMAN YEAR, I have been in love with Fetien Mihirät. She has always been on mind, even when I was with other girls, many of whom would throw themselves at me. My charisma. My manliness. My blackness. I could score hookups with my big smile and muscles, and a cool nod.

But I was always thinking of Fetty, even though I knew she was in love with Kevin. Or maybe because of it. Not out of some weird jealousy or some competitiveness or even because I wanted the one who didn't want me. No, I just wanted someone to want me for the same reasons Fetty wanted Kevin. His intelligence, his sensitivity—that's what attracted Fetty to Kevin. No one I ever hooked up with cared that I aced AP tests or won geography bees. Or if they did, it just was a funny irony to point out. *Ha, he's actually really smart.* Ha, you're *actually* kind of racist.

But Fetty never cared about how popular and *irresistible* I was. Her attraction to Kevin was deeper, even if it was futile. I never saw Kevin show interest in anyone.

I cherished her, and Kevin, too much to ever make a move. Almost like she was a rare, wild creature to be watched but not owned. My attraction to Fetty was the reason I hung around after building the latrines, watching over her. It was part of the reason that I instantly sprung at the men with guns who were attempting to rape her. I didn't want to see such an innocent and beautiful person destroyed, no matter the cost to me or the tribe. So, I attacked the guards and took the blows and everything else that followed, changing me into something the opposite of innocent and pure.

I have watched Fetty leave the tribe on her long excursions. Coming back, every time a bit different. She is still beautiful, but she, too, is no longer innocent. I look up at the new Fetty, standing on the hood of the Humvee, armed and menacing. Now I know what she was hunting: answers. And she is coming to collect on my sins.

"Michael! How could you?"

I let out a heavy sigh. I glance at Anahita. She watches Fetty with a calm, almost amused look on her equanimous face. I slide my hand out from under hers and open the door. By the time my feet are on the ground, Fetty is off the vehicle and towering in front of me.

I stand and face her.

"Did you do it?" she asks, looking up at me with a burning intensity.

I start to feel terror. More than anything, I don't want Anahita to hear Fetty recount my crimes, even with her weak grasp of English. *They came for my daughters.* But maybe she already knows.

I reach out to hold Fetty's shoulder, to guide her back so I can shut the door and prevent Anahita from hearing the conversation. She knocks my hand away with an animalistic fierceness that actually hurts. Ha, I actually might be kind of sexist.

"Did you sell—"

"Yes," I confess. "We did it so we could surv—"

She hits me, hard, across my face with the butt of her rifle. Her crows start to spin as I fall to the ground. *Everything* is spinning as I look up at the sky. The circling crows seem to glide faster and faster, like sharks moving in the for the kill.

Warm liquid collects in the back of my throat. I roll over and spit blood out of my mouth while my nose releases a steady, crimson stream. I try to collect my thoughts. To stop the whirling,

I concentrate on watching the bright, red drops fall into the fresh, white snow.

Heavy clops ring through the air. I am not sure if the sound is ringing in my ears and wonder if this is another fucking concussion. Sorry, Dad.

I glance up from the bloody snow. On the dirt road, I see horse hooves, surrounded by the human legs of an assembled crowd. I start to get up.

"What the fuck is going on?" Eva yells.

I gather my strength and place my hands on the running board of the Humvee. I slowly stand. Anahita is still staring at me with that amused, calm look. Does nothing shock her? Her calmness is catching. I shake my head like an aged detective who's getting too old for this shit.

I shut the door and look toward Eva. She has her rifle pointed at Fetty.

Fuck. Eva is very bright and probably already knows what is going on. And she's cold-blooded enough to kill Fetty to keep our secret.

"Eva, it's fine," I garble. My choice of words sounds comical through a mouthful of blood.

Eva looks at me and shakes her head, as if giving me a warning. Suddenly, I am glad Charlotte, Spencer, and others have gathered around. Eva is cold-blooded but not crazy. She won't kill Fetty in front of people without just cause.

But while Eva's giving me the stink-eye, Fetty slowly edges closer toward her and the horse. Then she pounces. She drops her rifle and sprints, nearly on all fours, at Eva, a bush streaking through the grass. My heart starts racing. Eva just got her cause; she can fire and claim self-defense.

The distance seems too far, but Fetty shields her body between the horse's head and Eva's rifle. Eva can't get a clean shot.

Fetty closes the gap remarkably fast. Eva tries to maneuver the horse to point her rifle at Fetty, but it's too late. Fetty darts to the other side of the horse's head. Eva aims her rifle on the other side, but Fetty jukes back, then jumps up and pulls Eva down off her horse.

Eva hits the ground with a thump and a sickening wheeze. Relentless, Fetty presses her knee to Eva's gasping chest. Her knife is out and against Eva's throat.

"Who is this girl?" I wonder. She is no longer the innocent person I cherished and sought to protect. What did she turn into in the wilderness, alone, with her murder of crows? Suddenly, I understand why the crows follow her. I also understand why the other base has never found us while I waited like a stoic and useless guard in the Humvee. It wasn't just answers she was hunting.

Fetty bends down closer to Eva, face to face. Through a clenched jaw, loud enough for everyone to hear, she seethes: "I know what you did!"

9

ME TOO

(Fetien)

~

The calmness of Spencer and Cisco makes me feel uneasy. Did I overreact? Why did I jump so easily to violence? There is a change —no, more like a growth—inside of me that feels both foreign and natural at the same time. Almost like coming to America and being a stranger, but familiar with a culture I saw in movies and TV shows. I was split between two worlds, America and Ethiopia, not really belonging in either. And the Americans split me further: white people see me as black; black people see me as African.

And now, I seem to be split between good and evil, and not really belonging to either.

We are all gathered in the LDS temple. Homemade benches have been moved into a crooked circle on the old, piled rugs. I thought it was forbidden for non-Mormons to enter, but Spencer says that without formal dedication by an LDS bishop it is just a place of worship, a chapel for everyone. Still, I nervously look around for any crucifixes or pictures of our Lady Mary that will frown down on me and the person I have become. I see nothing.

"Now, Fetty, can you please explain what the heck is going on?" Spencer asks.

Spencer and Cisco talked me down when I had Eva pinned. They separated us into the temple, away from the rest of the tribe.

Michael is here with Lupina and Charlotte, tending to his broken nose. They have snow wrapped in cloth held against his swollen face. I look at him and feel a tinge of remorse, until I visualize what those girls must be going through right now. The guilt is gone. I look at Eva, sitting across from me in the temple. She is watching me liked a cornered animal. I stare her down, too. Do you even kill, bro? I think.

"Fetty? Are you there?"

I turn to Spencer and force a calm look on my face.

"You can't come into Caxm and attack people. This is a peaceful place, and those days...those days are over."

I scoff and hear Eva and Michael snort at the same time. Maybe we understand the specter of violence better than the rest of them. Lupina gently wipes blood from Michael's lips and tears from his cheeks.

"Now, we appreciate the meat you bring us, but that behavior will not be tolerated."

"What do you have to say for yourself?" Cisco follows up.

We appreciate the meat you bring us? I feel like I do not belong, again. Like I am some foreigner coming in for the occasional trade. If they only knew what I have been doing out there, what I have become to protect them.

I look around the yurt, from Cisco to Spencer to Michael, Charlotte, and Lupina. I settle on Eva as she gives me a warning stare.

"This is not a peaceful place," I start. "Caxm wasn't founded on *sharing* and caring. It was founded on taking and enslaving."

"Now, we all did some bad things, out of self-defense, necessary thin—" Spencer tries to mansplain, but I cut him off.

"Kevin...Eva and Michael sold Lily, Becky, and Kelly into sexual slavery. They traded them to the militia for the sheep that helped sustain us."

Everyone is shocked. Eva starts to protest, but I keep going. I push through their whines.

"And then...and then! Kevin instructed the Afghani militia to attack the base and take the rest of the teenagers after we left."

Eva shuts up. I look at her and Michael. They seem surprised. At least they were not involved in that terrible crime. The wheels are turning in their heads to see if this adds up. It does.

"This is bullshit," Eva finally says. She does not sound convincing. She looks like she is still contemplating Kevin's other great crime and whether she can be implicated.

"Michael, is it? Is it bullshit?" I demand.

Michael stands up and brushes Charlotte and Lupina's care away.

"She's right. We sold the girls." His voice sounds throaty and deep through the pooling blood. "This village was not founded on peace. This village, this world, is an evil place and always has been."

"Michael," I say. "You are responsible for your own choices no matter what the world has become. Just like you chose to save me from rape, you chose to sell those girls. You are complicit. You are a rapist."

Michael closes his eyes tight. He shakes his head. More drops of blood escape out of his nose and fall to the rug and blend in with the dark red fabric.

"Fetty, you don't know what they did to me," he says. He opens his eyes, and they are welling tears. He stares at me with such pain and sorrow.

"Michael, we were there. We do know," Lupina says. "But that doesn't justify what you did."

"No. You weren't there! You don't know what they did to me!" His voice is cold and hard but strangely almost childlike. "After..."

"Oh, no, Michael. Not you. Not you, too," Charlotte pleads. She moves close to Michael and wraps her arms around him. She buries her head into his chest like a child hiding. "I'm sorry we didn't save you sooner." Her words are muffled and soft. Michael encloses her in his arms.

After a long pause, Michael continues over Charlotte's child-like cries. "They broke me. They broke the buck."

"They sought to teach me a lesson. And they did: the world is full of bad men. Fetty, you understand this as well. And now I know, I was put on this earth to remove those bad people. I am good at it. And you are good at it, too, Fetty. That's why we've been safe all these months. I figured it out. You've been out there killing those soldiers looking for us, keeping us safe, and you know what? They deserved the death you dealt. They were bad people."

"But Michael — we sold girls, and killed...killed so many men —how do you know *we* are not the bad people?" I ask, more to myself than him.

We stare at each other for a long time. We are both completely different from the kids that boarded the plane in Denver. He went from an always smiling teenager to my savior to a slave trader. I went from a shy girl to a near victim to a killer of men. *And you are good at it, too, Fetty.*

"I guess we're all bad people," he finally manages to say.

"Now, hold on—" Spencer says.

"I've had enough of this shit," Eva interrupts. She stands up and starts stalking back and forth. "Congrats. We're all bad people. But at least we're alive bad people. And we wouldn't be if it wasn't for Kevin and what we did. Don't forget that. But what I want to know, Fetty, is how you knew? How did you find out?"

"We would not be alive without Lupina and what she did. Do not forget that!" My only thank you for her taking charge when we reached the valley instead of letting Eva, Annie and I barge into the village with brandished guns to dictate our way. Lupina took Eva's dictionary and learned one word as she marched toward the orchard followed by the herd of sheep. The word, *caxm:*

pronounced like Sam but meaning share in Tajiki. And the village took us in as their own.

"Yeah, right, the village was ours whether they *shared* it or not. Now answer the fucking question. How did you know what happened to the girls? Did you beat it out of Michael?" She gives Michael a disdaining glare before moving her scorn back to me. She thinks she has found a weakness. She will not relent. Maybe she, too, suspects Pax of being a traitor and thinks we are communicating.

"It is…a long story," I say.

"Tell it," Cisco says. Everyone is watching me. I look back at Lupina. She is on the edge of her seat. Everyone wants to know if the long story includes news about Kevin and Pax.

"Michael is right. I have been killing men, killing lots of men. The other base, the one that attacked us on the road, they never stopped looking for us. And the bodies, the bodies obtained…." I think of the four dead soldiers picked apart by crows and wolves while I watched from my rocky throne. Did I enjoy that?

"I figured the game of hide and seek in the forest was eventually going to end with me dead. So, I decided to go for the heart. I enacted a plan Kevin planted with me before he left with Pax. When he gave me a map, he also gave me a key to the major's room. He said I could sneak back in and frack whoever was occupying it to cause chaos."

"Wait, what's fracking? And who was occupying it? I thought you said the militia took over the base," Lupina asks.

"Fracking is secretly blowing up your leader with a grenade. The militia did take over the base after we left, but soon after, the American soldiers from Afghanistan came up and attacked the militia. They took over. The ones on the side of the coup in America are now in charge of the base. Many teenagers survived, so the soldiers knew what Kevin did, and what we all did to the National Guard, so they kept hunting us.

"But without material support from America, the base has gone bad, decayed into something tribal and rotten. They, too,

enslaved the remaining teenagers. So, per Kevin's plan, I snuck onto the base and into the major's room. I fracked him with grenades, made it look like it was an inside job to cause infighting for his spot on the throne. Then they would be too busy and broken to hunt for us. Before I killed him, he told me all this. And…"

I take a long breath. I don't know any other way to say it. So, I just do.

"And he told me Pax killed Kevin because he sold the girls into slavery."

The quiet during my story disappears. Cisco, Spencer, and Eva are up, barraging me with questions.

I ignore them all and focus on Lupina. She is not talking, but her eyes plead with me.

"I do not know," I say. I try to get the image of the *figure-Y* out of my head, a thought I do not want to pass on to her. "…if Pax is still alive."

She stands up and somehow everyone stops talking. They all look at Lupina.

"I know Pax. I know his heart. He went to try and save those girls. And I am going to find him and help him. This tribe means nothing otherwise." She turns to leave. Her words are strong and final. I imagine Lupina, the kindest and most innocent among us, in the wilds outside the valley. Even without all the soldiers hunting us, the forest is still a very dangerous place.

She reaches the flap of the yurt with Charlotte trailing behind.

"Hey," Eva calls out. Lupina looks back over her shoulder. "You better hope I don't find him first."

And now the forest is even more dangerous.

10

THE TRIBE

(Michael)

～

I knew it was wrong, but I followed Kevin anyway. We were caught up in the battle, and I just had my first kill. I kicked open the door to the corporal's room and charged in. He grabbed his pistol and jumped up. I closed the distance, crouched down, sprung and jammed Kevin's knife through his heart. I hit him so hard I pinned the knife into the wall behind him while he fired his final, desperate shots into the opposite wall.

The rush was unlike anything I ever felt before, pure adrenaline and euphoria. The person who tortured me was now dead, at my hand. I was safe; he was gone. Everything that followed felt like a long orgasmic blur.

Kevin and Eva fired their weapons at the corporal's henchman as they filed into the hallway to investigate the pistol shots. We cleared the rest of the rooms and cordoned off the girls with Eva at their guard, while Kevin and I joined the rest of the battle.

I had the corporal's pistol and hurried to follow Kevin. A firefight was breaking out by the motor pool. A chorus of gunshots shouted back and forth. Kevin was bold, unflinching; he bolted straight toward the gunfire.

We reached the hangar that housed the motor pool. Enemy soldiers were firing into the building where our friends were holed up. I flinched as I heard a loud explosion from within the building. But Kevin didn't hesitate. He charged at the group of soldiers amassed around our friends, closing the noose.

They didn't see us coming. Their backs were to us. Kevin started firing, and I followed. We lit them up. Pinned, with bullets flying from behind and in front, many of the soldiers died but the rest surrendered. They were just like us in many ways. They didn't want to be there. They didn't want to risk their lives or take others'. Knowing they were surrounded, they yelled "surrender!" then put down their weapons and raised their hands. They approached us sheepishly, many only still wearing their underwear, shuffling forward with hands up and heads down.

But we killed them anyway.

I was still lost in the euphoria of the battle, in the sweetness of my revenge on the corporal. I didn't want to think much about it. Later I made excuses: they were all involved in my torture; all part of the killing of the professional soldiers; I was caught in the heat of the battle; I was just following Kevin's lead.

Evil isn't a genetic disposition. It's not the mark of the beast, or an indelible, dark stain on your soul. Evil is a learned addiction that takes hold faster than any drug. It's something you get used to and make excuses for, just like a junky. They deserved to die; it was us or them; just another hit, man.

So, I could go from a justified revenge killing to the murder of surrendering soldiers to the selling of innocent girls into slavery in just a matter of hours. Just another hitman.

Kevin knew this. He knew that I would seek revenge for what was done to me and this could be parlayed into doing terrible things. That's why I was chosen for the mission to sell the girls. But he never told me about what happened to the base after we left. Did he not think my evil addiction would go that far? His did. He went from orchestrating an attack on the base to selling girls into slavery to betraying hundreds of fellow teenagers as pawns in a deadly struggle.

When Fetty told the part of the story about Kevin handing the base over to the militia, I knew it was true. I knew he had it in him. Where did his evil addiction start? Was it something he learned while being alone in the forest, much like Fetty, now? Or did it start sooner, before the catastrophe, with his abusive mom who abandoned him in death?

Regardless, I can see why Pax killed him. Like someone blaming their bad behavior on the drugs, evil is also just an excuse. But it wasn't to Pax. Is it to me? What about Eva or Fetty?

I LOOK at Eva and Fetty. After Lupina and Charlotte left, they continued to stare each other down.

Finally, Fetty breaks the silence. She looks at Cisco and Spencer. "Lupina is right, again. This tribe—The Tribe of Iodine Wine—this village of Caxm, it means nothing if we earned our peace though evil." On the word evil, she returns her glare at Eva.

"You are such a fuck—" Eva starts.

"Shut up!" Fetty commands. There is something deadly and direct in her voice that contradicts the sweet, shy Fetty we have always known. Almost instinctively, my flight reflexes fire. For a split second, I feel absolute fear. I think it's probably because she just broke my nose, but I look around the room, at Cisco, Spencer, and even Eva. I can tell they feel it, too. Their eyes are wide and scared like prey underneath a predator's pounce.

"But Lupina is wrong to chase the ghost of those girls," she continues with her voice now calm and rational. "Our redemption resides in the base. There are hundreds of teenagers, our peers, who are trapped and enslaved there. We need to save them, to save our souls."

"The base? You're going to attack the base?" Eva asks. She starts to laugh.

"We are. We all are. We owe it. This is our one good deed, our Covenant of Mercy, to make up for all the bad we have done."

"Yeah, right. I told you where I'm going. Cisco and I are going after Pax. He killed the only person we owe anything to."

"Eva, Fetty, hold on. No one is going anywhere, including Lupina, including you two," Cisco says. "We took an oath to protect the tribe, those teenagers didn't. Pax did, but he chose to leave."

"And besides, Ezra is pregnant now. My number one priority is keeping her safe," Spencer says.

Fetty and Eva ignore the boys and keep staring each other down. Fetty walks toward Eva, then brushes by her.

"Good luck in the forest, Eva. I will keep one eye open, looking for you," Fetty says as she slips past the flap.

I FEEL NAKED, exposed. This is the farthest away from the guns I have been in months. My head hurts. My nose is broken. I leave the yurt. Eva is calling Cisco a pussy and saying something about never getting hers again. I feel sick and retreat to the Humvee.

The sun is out. The snow glistens and shines as it melts. The bright, reflective light hurts my head even more.

I open the door and lumber back in. Anahita is still waiting for me, still smiling. I sit next to her, and she puts her hand back on top of mine and continues her hum. We watch the village together.

Lupina and Charlotte are talking to Jaden. He looks upset but then just shakes his head and starts to gather his gear. He comes back and at least is carrying a rifle. Charlotte is folding up canvas into a bag that will serve as a tent and a backpack. She slips her big scissors into a specially made holster on her hip.

Lupina is unarmed, of course. She is gathering food: smoked meats, nuts and dried fruits. For three people, it looks like enough food for two or three weeks. She also takes some medicine out of her medical bag and leaves it with another nurse for the village to have in their absence. The gesture is depressing, not just for the kindness of thinking about the village, but for the efficiency of not wanting to waste the precious medicine if they don't make it back.

Fetty leaves one of the storehouses with some dried food supplies, too. Then she puts on her camouflage and picks up her rifle. She walks past my Humvee. She stares at me then shakes her head. She goes into the other Humvee and removes a couple of boxes of ammo for her rifle.

She joins my old friends, and I start to feel some hope. But she just removes a map tucked under her cords, next to her breasts, and hands it to Charlotte. She points to a couple of spots on the map, then marches off into the forest without looking back, alone, with her crows.

Soon after, Charlotte, Lupina, and Jaden follow but split off in a different direction, up toward the mountain ridge they scaled to enter the village a few months ago.

Who is my tribe? Is it the people who watched me get whipped, then saved me—in many ways, too late? Too much time passed between the cracks of the whip and the breaking of the chain, and I turned into a wraith devoid of any tribal belonging, including the Tribe of Iodine Wine. Or am I automatically a tribe member with Eva, Fetty, Jaden, and Danny, because of the color of our skin? But who would I choose between Eva and Fetty?

I remember my dad used to tell stories about tribes. "Not our fucking tribe," he would say, many times, when gathered or on the phone with his football buddies from CU. The motto would be blurted to any teammate, not just the black ones. I didn't know what he meant for many years, but I felt excluded, in a way that seemed impossible to overcome, because he wouldn't let me play football, and thus banned me from his precious tribe.

I was eavesdropping from the basement while he hosted a high-stakes poker game, and I found out what ticked him off. It was the fanatical fans of their football teams; they went to the games and screamed and sang fight songs; they wore the jerseys; they exalted the players on the field but in many ways, the players, like my dad and his friends, found the adulation weird, almost a form of theft. It was the players who trained relentlessly, who bashed their bodies (and brains) for a hard-fought victory. But the fans, the men who came and got to share in the spectacle of manhood as spectators, got to share in the victory, too, even though they weren't part of the team, despite the bullshit about the twelfth player.

The story my dad told, his disdainful view of fans nearly broke my heart at the time, because I knew I would never be part of this tribe of players. That's why I was never a fan of watching sports, because of his opinion of those glory thieves.

But what I thought about a lot, from the secluded seat of the Humvee, was the fake tribal belonging that we ascribed to, even outside of sports, in concerts and politics. I never understood how poor, white racists could be so against poor black people. How can they carry an invisible membership card to a tribe whose leadership exploited their ignorance to rip them off and keep them and other poor people down?

False tribes are dangerous. Is my overwatch of Caxm and the Tribe of Iodine Wine a worthy path, or am I just another thieving spectator? My friends are heading into a perilous forest to save Pax, to wash away our sins, and I am hiding like a little boy listening to grown men tell stories of battle and victory.

"I need to leave," I finally say to Anahita.

She gives me a curious look with a canine-like turn of her head.

I point to my heart, to me. "I go," I say. I sign my fingers walking away, toward the forest.

"I need food." I mimic the universal act of eating. My fingers grasp imaginary morsels that I shovel into my mouth. "For three weeks." I give her the three sign. "OK?"

"OK," she responds. She pats my leg, then slowly turns and opens the door. She slides to the ground as her humped back cascades over the worn seat. She turns and gathers her teapot and cups. She looks up at me and smiles.

"Three. Food. Go," she repeats, then nods.

"Three, food, go," I respond.

Anahita waddles toward the village with her tea pot swinging to her odd cadence.

I jump out of the vehicle and prepare the rest of my supplies, then go to the back of the Humvee and pick up the two rocket boxes of ammunition connected by a thick length of rope. I string the rope across my shoulders and lift the ammo.

The multiple reps of squats I used with the boxes and rope will pay off. I carry the bullets up to the front of Humvee and grab the big gun.

Everyone watches me as I trudge across the orchard with my weapon and hanging boxes of bullets.

Anahita finds me in the middle of the village. I am relieved to stop for a second on my already short journey. The ammo will be a heavy burden to bear, but not as much as unloading it.

"Husband's," Anahita says to me and hands me what looks like a thick felt robe. She makes a gesture of holding her hand up high. She stretches her scoliosis-bent back as far as she can. He hijab slips back as she tries to stand up straight and reveals a wool cap, inlaid with jewels. Her gesture must mean, "he was as big as you." She smiles a devilish smile. as if remembering her strong, virile husband.

I fold the robe and run it across my shoulders. The thick fabric will offer a nice cushion to the heavy rope weighted with boxes of bullets.

Anahita offers me a satchel. She lifts it up, and I kneel and bend my neck. I feel like I am being knighted or given a medal. I slide one shoulder over the strap. The leather bag is heavy with food and a water-skin.

I straighten up and say, "*Sipos.*" Thank you in Tajiki. At least I learned this word.

She reaches up and holds my cheek in her warm hand. "Find peace," she says.

I want to laugh at the thought considering the dangerous task I am about to take on, but I just return the salutation. "Find peace."

FOURTH STORY

CARRION CROWS

Fetien

FETIEN

IV

1

QUEEN OF THE WORLD

~

I stomp back into the forest, away from Caxm and a shocked Eva, humbled and scared with fear in her eyes, primal, dangerous, a cornered animal ready to strike. I turn back around and scan my exit for any sneaking followers. The way Eva would talk behind people's back, always gossiping to me in high school, means she would be the type of person to shoot you in the back.

But only the crows stalk behind me. I trudge backward on my familiar and worn trail, watching the approaches, watching the birds swirl around the trees, listening for them to call out a danger.

I left a map with Lupina and Charlotte and departed to pursue my own crazy mission. I no longer need my map; I know where I am going, and I go alone, as always. Returning to the base, to where the adventure started.

"Like the hero's journey in reverse," I yell at my crows and Caxm in the distance, then chuckle at my odd outburst.

Not a villain's journey, I hope, just a hero unwanted and unassisted. But whatever. When you are black, foreign, and female, the hero's journey is three steps harder, and I must walk it backward.

But I turn back around and exchange my backward bumbling for my quick prance through the forest. I pick up my pace and start to sprint through the trees. The familiar feeling of wind on my face, the branches scratching at me, the ka-kaws of my birds feels comfortable, but I feel lessened, weaker from the past few days. My body is tired and my mind exhausted.

The days are starting to catch up with me, both the adrenaline-filled physicality of fracking the leader and the emotional drain of dealing with what he said, and in many ways, the subsequent death of our tribe. Congrats, I guess, dead-leader-guy. You fracked our people as much as I did yours.

Can we recover from the truth of what we did? The selling of the girls. The betraying of the rest of the teenagers. The brutal battle for the base. My forest killings. Fault lines are drawn by the horror of what we did and the fact that some of us think it was necessary. Was it? Did we need to do what we did? Did I need to become a killer of men?

Can my family's tradition of The Covenant of Mercy, the one good deed in Mother Mary's name, erase all the bad deeds I have done?

The ambiguity of it all is a mess I want to avoid. Maybe that is why I left by myself. I did not join with Lupina, Charlotte, and Jaden to find Pax or stay behind at Caxm to wrest control from Eva and convince the tribe to gain redemption, to pay the toll, by attacking the base and saving the teenagers left behind. Maybe I just like the simplicity and finality of a suicide mission: save the teenagers by myself or die trying.

Or maybe I just prefer to be alone.

MY FIRST YEAR in America was the most alone I ever felt until now. I studied proper Queen's English in the years leading up to our emigration from Ethiopia. I could communicate. I just didn't.

I understood the words, but sometimes missed the true meanings, missed the full meanness in their exclusion and taunts. So, I went into a shell, too unsure of my English to answer their words with rebukes.

At lunch, I always sat alone, against the fence of the middle school yard so no one could sneak up on me. The ghetto girls had recently invented a new game. They liked to hunt me down and scare me. Their only weapon was words. Well, one word: "Spearchucker!"

They would sneak down the halls like hunters stalking their prey. Over-exaggerated Elmer Fudd movements leading to a jump out around corners or pounce from behind while yelling "Spearchucker." To their credit, they got and appreciated the irony of hunting someone with a taunt about that person being a hunter. And now, the greatest irony: I have become a very deadly huntress.

From the window in her classroom, my science teacher would watch me at lunch, scared and alone, with my back against the fence. Never truly alone though, since I had books for company. My quick command of English may have missed the idioms of my bullies, but I could comprehend the vernacular of classical literature. My eyes danced back and forth between page and the playground plains of my tormentors.

But, perceiving me to be alone, my science teacher took sympathy on me. One day, the teacher asked if I would like to spend recess with her, in her classroom.

She asked coyly, "Fetien, would you mind helping me set up our next project at lunch?"

I knew this was just an excuse to connect, to help me, but part of me was so in need of a friend that I played along.

For the next couple of months, I helped set up projects, or read while she graded papers, or helped her grade papers, or just sat and watched inappropriate sitcoms with her. One day, after a particularly hard taunting about my African-ness by fellow females of African descent, my wonderful science teacher started a lecture for me on evolution, one of her favorite topics.

"Fetien," she started. "Did you know you are the Queen of the World?"

I looked up from my book. In Ethiopia, a relative once rambled on about some distant claim to royalty. I wondered my teacher was talking about my semi-noble family name.

"Those girls who descended from West Africa," she said with a nod to the window and the field beyond. "The white people that, maybe, look down on you. Even people far off in China and Japan. Everyone descended from your people."

I looked at her, perplexed and curious as she carried an old anthropology book over to me. She opened it up to a hand-drawn map on a page, brown and worn with age. She pointed to places near the Horn of Africa, near where I was born.

"Earliest humans evolved here. They evolved to their surroundings of East Africa, and it is imprinted on all of us. It's why we have a biological aesthetic, um, an attraction to rolling plains, to savannahs of green grass, to lone trees on a hill. Even the majestic animals of Africa like elephants and lions have a special draw for us. Because we evolved with them.

"But do you know the most interesting part? They evolved with us, too. They knew how to survive with us. Do you ever wonder why we don't see elephants and lions all around the world? They used to be worldwide, you know, until fairly recently. But most were killed off. It seems, for all its dangers, the Kings and Queens of Africa still know how to get along with majestic beasts. They are responsible hunters. Because a true, rightful ruler is one that can flourish with all.

"Be a rightful queen, Fetien. Don't separate yourself from the others. One day, you will be a doctor, and you may need to save the same people that hurt you, that hurt others," she finished. And that was the end of her months-long lesson. She released me back into the wilds of middle school with the quiet confidence of a one-day doctor who needed to fit in and gently get along with all.

. . .

AFTER HOURS and hours of running, I reach my nest tired and ready to collapse. My mind is boggled with the heavy decision I must make. I need to choose the right path. I can join my friends to find Pax. I can go back to Caxm and become the queen I was meant to be, the leader the military and science teacher knew I always had in me. Or I can continue my impossible mission, my one good deed, to the base by myself. But I feel dirty, tainted. I have killed too many people, and liked it too much to be an effective leader.

But why, I often wondered, did the military select me as leader? I take off my costume and place her against my legs. I am still breathing heavy from the long, frantic run. After months alone in the wilderness, I know why I was selected. The key to success is the ability to suffer, to wallow in pain, fear, guilt, and doubt but not change your course; instead, use the suffering to drive you forward, to accomplish the impossible because failing is not as bad as existing in mediocrity. Sleeping with one eye open, in the dark, amongst the trees and soldiers and ghosts has strengthened me more than any training.

I glance around my home, at the supplies, at my timeline of strings and cord still stretching across the small clearing. The decorations, I think, will probably outlast me, serve as archeological find to whoever stumbles upon it and my strung-out timeline, maybe a piece of evolutionary history in a far-off future.

Exhausted, I lay down in a nest of feathers and grass, scavenged clothes and pine needles. I place the costume over me, positioned so I can still see through a gap in the outcroppings of boulders, laying on my side, with one eye scanning the opening and blurry horizon beyond washed in an acidic orange sunset. I fall asleep to the sound of my rapid heartbeat and the fluttering crows.

2
THE 1 PERCENT

~

I startle and spurt and wake up from a nightmare. I was back home, back in my childhood in Ethiopia. On the anniversary of my uncles' deaths, my mother and her sisters held a coffee ceremony for their fallen brothers. Taken in the Ethiopian Civil War before my time, they were still revered, still cherished, and one of my responsibilities was to help prepare and pour them coffee.

I always thought it was spooky to provide our beloved beverage for no one. To let it sit and steep untouched. I imagined the mixing apparitions of steam and the smoke from the coals dancing upward with the ghosts of my uncles. My elders treated them as if they were real, so I always expected them to come to life and scare me as I poured the coffee.

In my dream, my uncles, pieced together in my mind from their numerous photos, sat there waiting for me to pour the coffee, but their skin was ashen and decomposing. I was scared to continue the ceremony as they sat and looked down at me with stern judgement. They had the young faces of their interrupted youth, but still looked ancient with death and decay.

"*Imebêti,*" an uncle said with a wave of his decrepit hand, motioning to the empty cups. I lifted the *jebena* and slowly poured. In my dream, the coffee seemed too thick and flowed out a shocking red in a black and white scene.

I jolted back at the blood, thinking I have disgraced my uncles, but they only laughed out loud, hearty laughs that mixes with the real-life, early morning ka-kaws of my crows and wakes me.

I blink, looking around my nidus, my familiar nest within a nest. Then I try to dampen my fear, focusing instead on the tangible knowledge I have of my family, rather than the myth of my dream.

Although I never met my uncles, my family—from parents to grandparents to surviving aunts—all had shrines to them in their American homes, too. I remember staring at their pictures framed in incense smoke and flowers. These people who died at an age slightly older than I am now, but in a time that seems like forever ago.

As teenagers, they were pulled into a local warlord's army during the civil war. When the war spread its terror to our village, my uncles deserted the army to escort my family to the safety of Somalia. One died during the escape from the militia. One died during the exodus. And one died in another bout of retribution, near the end of the war, after my family was safe and he thought he was, too.

The unknown brothers of my mother died as teenage boys fighting in a civil war that ravaged my country for more years than they lived. A civil war whose lifespan bore many babies but even more deaths. The surviving family reminded me time and time again that the uncles sacrificed so their siblings, including my mom, could make it out alive. "We made it to America, because of them," was the oft said mantra. Thus, my altruistic and childless uncles replicated their genes, in me, too.

. . .

I PUSH off my costume and rest her against the boulder. I stand up and do an early morning stretch. For some reason, my path seems so sure now. I know where I am going. I also know I will not need my camouflage. Let her rest here, in my own shrine to the Tribe of Iodine Wine.

Piled against other boulders are the extra weapons and supplies I gathered from the soldiers I killed. Sprinkled on the ground are the feathers from my murder of crows. The long cord still strings across, ornamented with the knots I used to mark the moves of Kevin, Pax, Michael, and Eva. Despite the surety of my choice, what connection do I really share with these people, my tribe and the teenagers I am willing to risk my life to save? Should I sacrifice for them the way my uncles did for me and my family.

The crows are stirring around, hopeful for a fruitful day.

"Wait, just wait, my pretties," I tell them, then shake my head with the realization that I am excited, too. I jump up on a rock and start a lecture for my eager birds:

"We share the same number of genetic traits with an aunt or uncle as we do with a grandparent: a 25 percent intersection of alleles," I say. "You see, from an evolutionary perspective, an aunt or uncle has the same personal stake in keeping a niece alive as a grandparent does, to save their direct descendent. This kin selection, according to my beloved biology classes, is one of the reasons we evolved such esteemed traits as compassion and sacrifice."

I jump down of the rock and start to gather my stuff, guns, a bottle of rubbing alcohol.

"A childless uncle who sacrifices himself in war to save a clan that contains four nieces has replaced himself. Add siblings or children to the equation, at a 50 percent overlap, then he needs to save two to replicate his genes. Eight first cousins will also do, or any hodgepodge, say, two cousins, a niece and sister.

"The selflessness traits of a sacrificing uncle are more likely to occur in his surviving kin and be passed on, propagating even if he does not survive or have children because the clan wins, survives. So, in many ways, our superior social evolution It due to our aunts and uncles, they made humans into Kings and Queens of the World because they propagate the powerful traits of altruism, communication, and intelligence."

I grab all the bullets in my possession and fill my satchel with my supplies. I holster my pistol then pick up my rifle and walk out of my hideout and down the hillock. I pass the picked skeletons of four of my enemies and start to run more calculations in my mind as the crows swirl above me.

Jogging at an easy pace, I continue my lecture to the attentive crows. "If you take any two random strangers, generally their overlap of alleles is around 1 percent. I share 1 percent of my distinctive hereditary makeup with each member of The Tribe of Iodine Wine and each teenager left on the base. Despite our paltry genetic overlap, I am still going to sacrifice myself for them."

I stop, look up over the horizon like a soldier giving a pledge, a salute to duty.

"I need to save 101 strangers for my sacrifice to make evolutionary sense," I declare. I start my run toward the base.

However, the stark truth is this calculation requires counting the lives I have taken. I glance back at the skeletons. They are picked clean and melting into the grass and dirt. I put them there.

They, too, share the same 1 percent overlap with me. Maybe the real reason for my mission, for my impossible journey, is to counter the lives I have taken with ones saved. So, for my evolutionary calculus to truly work, I need to save, not only 101 people, but 101 more people than I have killed. But maybe this is not only what evolution demands of me, but also Mother Mary.

I head back to the base, alone, to fight for the 1 percent.

Yeah, and 1 percent is pretty much the odds I give myself to survive. There are probably 120 or so soldiers still left. I need to kill all of them. 1 percent sounds about right. Oh, but wait, if I slay 120 soldiers, then I need to save about 150 teenagers to still be on the right side of my moral, evolutionary calculus.

I stop and look up at the crows. "But wait. Do I want to count the soldiers in my evolutionary calculus?" The crows don't respond.

"Don't they carry the types of characteristics—depravity, murder, selfishness—that we want to weed out. Do I?"

I laugh, a brazen, loud and crazy laugh that sounds foreign. It rocks my throat and echoes off surrounded trees. I sense my loyal corvids, flying above me, turn their heads at the strange noise.

3

TRAITOR

~

The morning light welcomes me out of the forest as I streak across the plane. Instead of taking a cautious approach I just bolt straight for the small hole I dug under the fence. I pull the brush away, slide my rifle through, and crawl to the other side.

I lay in a prone position. My rifle scope scans the main barracks to my right. Things seem quiet, but I am nervous about a run to our old barracks during the daytime. I stay in the tall grass and wait. My bravado from before is tempered by the risky run ahead of me.

I keep watching for movement, for any opportunity to make the run. The main guard towers are all toward the front of the base and the main gate, but there are still too many people in plain sight. I can see guards at the teenagers' barracks and people walking around the main part of the base.

Suddenly, I hear a loud, sharp clang from one of the towers. An unconventional alarm that sets the soldiers to attention. They look toward the main gate with guns ready.

At first, I think the alarm is for me. I prepare to start firing at an coming onslaught and retreat under the fence, failing before I even started.

But the soldiers are not running my way. They are running toward the gate, armed and ready for a fight.

A Humvee is making its way toward the gate, then stops. Enthralled by the action, I lay mesmerized by their fear of the Humvee then realize this is my best opportunity to make it to our old barracks.

I take off in a sprint and keep watch on the Humvee and the gathered soldiers. A couple of Humvees from the base leave the motor pool and head toward the gate with their guns manned.

As I approach our old barracks, my heart starts to race. I see guards around the old teenagers' barracks. As the fracked leader said, the teens are enslaved and under tight control. I am too close to the guards, but they are too distracted by the commotion at the front of base. They do not look my way as I slip into the old MMM barracks.

Inside, I sweep my rifle around looking for danger like a SWAT member from a TV show. After assessing that the barracks are safe, I go to a window and focus my scope on the gate, curious about the commotion at the front of the base.

After what looks like a standoff, soldiers finally go up to the Humvee, rifles poised and start inspecting it. They even go inside and search the back. Then the two passengers are escorted out and walked through the gate under strict guard.

It seems almost comical, these two figures surrounded by a host of soldiers. Their arms are up in surrender as they are marched to the main part of the base. I focus my scope on the two prisoners. The one on my left is talking to a group of leaders like he knows them. Through the rifle, he looks young, white, kind of small and kind of familiar, but I cannot place him.

I move my scope to the other figure. I nearly fire my gun in shock and anger. On the other side of the scope, meeting with our enemies, stands Eva. She drove the Humvee. She brought this betrayal.

I start calculating the math for just springing outside and barreling toward her, about 300 yards away and twenty or so soldiers with their backs turned. I could probably make it past the buildings, halfway, before I am noticed, then I would need to start firing. Odds are I would not survive, but at 150 yards, I am pretty sure I would kill her, too.

It would be worth it. I will probably die soon anyway. Why not take her with me? But revenge is not why I am here. I am here to save the teenagers and help erase all the death I have caused.

But, how could she betray us? Then I realize the truth. Even more than Kevin, she showed her worth when she committed the heinous act of trading girls for sheep. She betrayed our gender when she exploited the girls. She betrayed her Jewish religion with the abetting of a war crime. She even betrayed our race by selling people into slavery. If she could do those things with no remorse, then she could betray our tribe. Loyalty flows like water, always settling even across the surface; to not show it to one group is to not show it for all. No wonder Eva is a traitor.

"Ah, and she is one of the Tribe you sacrifice for." I hear a voice, fluttering and ephemeral from above.

"She is not the one."

"Then who is? Who is this 1 percent you sacrifice and slave for?"

I shake my head and dispense with these thoughts. I should have known. I should have seen this three-piece move coming from her. That look in her eyes when I brought her down, not just fear but hate. Eva is so hung up on control of Caxm and our tribe that me throwing her to the ground and exerting power would make her do something this treasonous. Maybe she is a lot like Kevin. Maybe they were a better match anyway. They both would do anything to win, to gain control.

And maybe I am not violent enough? Maybe, when she

pointed her rifle at me, and I took her down off her high horse, I should have plunged my knife deep into her body. Mercy has its own risks.

THEY CONTINUE DEBATING. My scope is focused on Eva. She is pointing to the forest, toward where I approached the base. The movements look exaggerated, like she is explaining some great danger coming their way ending with what looks like a "number one" sign. The soldiers seem to laugh at her speech and doubt it with shakes of their heads. But she keeps pointing at the forest, then points to the leader's quarters that I blew up. Both her hands make an explosion sign before she points back to the forest.

Kevin made a remark once about spying on the headquarters of the base. I would give anything to hear what Eva was spewing out. Or maybe, if my crows were truly connected, truly symbiotic, they could spy for me and relay a message like out of some fantasy story.

But I can only watch her movements from afar. Eva mimics my big, kinky, afro hair. Her fingers float above her cowboy hat as if they are kneading bread. Then she points to her face. Her biracial face is the same lighter skin tone as mine. I do not need crows or Kevin's listening devices. I know what she is saying. She is warning the soldiers that I am coming for them. She not only betrayed the tribe, she betrayed me, her *Oreo Sister*. But she does not know how fast I am, or that I am already here.

Eva and her co-traitor walk back to their Humvee followed by a group of soldiers. They all get in. She turns the vehicle around. Other soldiers run around the fence and make their way into the forest where Eva pointed minutes before. More soldiers jump into the bases' Humvees that met Eva at the gate.

Three Humvees make their way up the torturous road, brimming with deceit and armed soldiers ready to steal our peace in the valley. Then it hits me: I no longer have a home. My worst fear has come to pass, even worse than her treachery toward me. I am completely alone. Caxm is lost. And mercy has its own risks.

4

ANOTHER BETRAYAL, ANOTHER DOOR

~

In all my planning, with my super-high government survival score and pre-med precision, I forgot to account for bathroom breaks. I snuck into the attic of our old barracks from a top bunk and trap door. Feeling my way through the dark, I crawled to the side of the roof facing the courtyard and soldiers' barracks. Then I stabbed a small hole into the roof, so I could case the base and plan my rampage.

My knife broke open a peephole, then I poked my fingers through to push away the old, withered pine branches that Cisco and Kevin had placed on the roof to absorb heat months earlier. Underneath the dying pines, I sat nested and focused, watching the base, noticing movement patterns, and mentally marking the route I would need to take from barracks to motor pool to where the National Guard slept.

I sat for a long time, legs crossed, butt and hands balancing me on a beam. My head leaned forward to peer through the hole, listening to the scratches and bickering of my crows on the roof above me. I sat in peace, almost in a state of meditation observing the workings of the dying base. My earlier anger was washing away, and I felt composed, ready to take on the task at hand in a rational frame of mind.

But after a long, quiet respite I suddenly realize I need to go to the bathroom. So used to squatting in the wilderness whenever I needed, I never even thought to grab a bucket or cut open an empty water tub.

Going to the latrines outside is out of the question. Even slipping down quietly to the main floor is fraught with risk. So, I leave my rifle and satchel, then climb back across the beams. Headlamps and flashlights are a long-gone luxury that died with their batteries. The only weak light comes in through the peephole and fades to black as I make my way to the other side.

I am about halfway across when my hand comes across something long, cold, and scaly. I instinctively pull back, having an irrational fear of surprising a snake in the dark. When I pull my hand back, I hear a soft scrape and thump on the ceiling. I reach down and grab the cord and give a tug. Something small, heavy, and familiar slides my way. I reach out and grab the cell phone, alien in the dark attic, an anachronistic device, alluring, calling me to press the familiar buttons.

I press the home button and to my surprise it lights up. A strong pull beckons me to call home or check a newsfeed for any sign of civilization and safety. But I know this is impossible. Somehow the cell phone still has life, but there is no signal, no connection.

I look down and see a tiny pinhole of light come up from the barracks below. I face the screen down to where the cell phone lay before and see a dust pattern. At the bottom of the silhouette, right where the microphone would rest, the pinhole beams a miniscule pillar of light.

I lift the light and scan the rest of the attic. Three cords stretch out and at the end of each serpentine body, lays the hydra-like heads of a cell phone.

Why? But I know why. On the day the helicopters went down, Kevin darted out of the barracks when Lupina told us that two other choppers were shot down. Then, scared children caught in a war in foreign lands, we all took an oath to protect one another. We drank water mixed with iodine and ceremonially became The Tribe of Iodine Wine. But Kevin was gone. He did not take the oath.

Kevin came back panicked and eager to leave. He told us that he placed listening devices at the headquarters. When he heard the news of the downed helicopters he went and listened to those "devices" and found out that America had broken out in civil war. The attack on our base's air power came from another American base, part of a coup in the United States. The goal of the upheaval was to take complete authoritarian control of America and violently suppress Muslim populations through our militarized colonies. The soldiers I am preparing to attack are from the same base in Afghanistan that shot down the helicopters.

But as soon as I picked up the connected phone, I knew Kevin did not bring spyware to Tajikistan. Those listening devices were gathered from our useless, discarded cell phones, but he also planted them in our barracks. His bunk was below the attic door, so he could easily access them.

Kevin was spying on us.

I throw the phone to the ceiling floor. It bounces and kicks up a plume of stale dirt then falls face down. The light presses into the ceiling and stretches out its toxic transmission like a monster that just will not die.

But I hear an echo reverberate up from the floor and through the attic door. A cacophony of sound builds on the bounce of the discarded phone and is joined by my beating heart. I recognize the sound: the boots of soldiers running through the barracks. They are looking for me.

Light twirls in the peephole with the movement below. Furious, boiling with anger at the betrayal by Eva and Kevin, so sick of humanity and my participation in this stupid dance, I stare down at the attic door.

The soldiers are over-turning abandoned beds, kicking over chests, making a ruckus loud with fear and fake bombast.

No, I want to play; I want join in the fun. My swan song is finally here. That's the thing about death. Once you've seen so much of it, dealt so much of it, it becomes welcome, boring even, deserved with its need to push it further.

I reach up to unshoulder my rifle ready to leap and crash through the attic door and see their surprised faces as I start firing away. But my rifle is by the crow's nest where I watched the base.

The sound from below is starting to die down and with it my need to kill. But my hand, as if my body is craving destruction reaches down and fondles my holstered pistol. Sensing the coming carnage, my crows are squawking through the roof, encouraging me to jump through the door.

I pull out the pistol, slowly turn off the safety and spring back on my haunches ready to pounce.

"No, *seti liji*." A soft motherly, voice tells me. "This is not why you are here."

The voice, foreign and familiar shocks me into a stupor more so than the surprising sounds from below. I stare at the attic down, dark and grey and inviting.

Still tense, still poised to leap like a leopard, pistol and teeth clenched, I keep staring at the door in the floor until I hear a slam and the soldiers exit our barracks.

5

SPEARCHUCKER

~

My blood still burns with anger. I am furious at the betrayals, at the loss of hope and connection to my tribe, at my weakness for not crashing through the attic door or hunting Eva down when I saw her. I just want to start the attack, just fire my gun in broad daylight and start the killings. My chances would have been nil, but in many ways, it would have been the right thing to do.

Instead, I relieved myself in the dark corner and snuck back to the nest underneath the pines and tin roof, underneath the crows, to wait and fume until night fell. Perfecting my plan over and over, running the stats and steps in my mind.

I look down at my handmade spear. The spear is made from a 2x4 broken off a bunk with my knife tightly wrapped around the end. Not the most aerodynamic weapon, but it will do. My fingers run down the hard, square angles of the shaft. The weapon is like the ones they made before the Battle of the Base, when only Kevin, Paco, and I had guns, and the rest of our tribe broke apart bunks and cut tin off the roof to make rough spears.

I use the butt of the spear to hold my weight as I bend over to stretch my hamstrings. My back and legs are sore from being in a crouched position. I have been stuck in the attic for over a day, but I have seen too much and done too little and this makes me eager and impatient to leave. I put the spear down and crouch my way to the small hole in the roof. I take another look around the base. It is completely dark, and I see very little movement. Still, I must wait until a later hour to increase the chances of everyone being asleep.

I finish doing some more yoga stretches while breathing in long, calm breathes, trying to ignore the smell. It is almost time. I start to shake my muscles awake, shake away the staleness of being stuck in this attic for twenty-four hours. I take one more careful look out of the hole in the roof and make my decision.

I slide from the hole in the ceiling and climb onto Kevin's deserted bunk bed. I reach back up and grab my rifle and my spear. A soft patter rolls through the empty barracks as I jump down to the floor. I look around the large hall and start to feel nostalgic, a longing for the friends I once had. I feel utterly alone. I cannot go back to Caxm—I know this now. And my chances of ever seeing Lupina, Charlotte, and Jaden again are next to nothing.

I play with the fantasy of making new friends on this base. Once I save the teenagers, I will be their heroine, their queen, right? I will be revered as a savior. I can finally get over this feeling of isolation.

Not a time for such a weak thought.

In full stalking mode, I glide out into the night and make my way to the far side fence that borders the plains. The ground descends toward the barrier. I run along this slight hill in a crouch.

When I finally make it to the backside of the motor pool, I collect myself while standing with my back to the big building. I slide my spear out and slowly make my way around to the other side. Before I get to the front of the building, I prepare myself. Two seconds. I take a few steps backward to ramp up my running start. Silence shrouds the base, and I embrace her cold warmth.

Above me, excited in anticipation, the crows launch off the buildings and hover closer to me. They swirl over my halo as I take off in a full-sprint.

I reach the corner of the motor pool and break hard right. My feet are light and soft, producing little sound. My grip hardens on the bulky spear. My body is pressing forward. I look up, ready to close the distance and impale the guard, but he is gone. I stop at the door. Is he inside? This is already going badly.

I glance toward the other side of the building and see a round butt sticking out. I listen closely and hear a man taking a piss. The sound stops, and I take off in my sprint again. He turns around and comes into full view.

I am still too far away when he sees me bearing down on him. He lifts his rifle, and I throw my spear. It flies at him awkwardly, but he is too scared to fire his gun. He tries to avoid the knife point. It glances off his turning shoulder and falls to the ground, heavy, sticking in with a thump.

I am airborne as the guard returns his attention to me. I clear his rifle and dropkick him in the face and chest. He flies backward and hits the ground hard. I land on my knees, scoop up the spear then jump again.

My feet land on both sides of the guard, and I plant the spear hard in his heart like I am claiming new land. There is a loud crack when the knife plunges through the heart and the 2x4 breaks the sternum. Blood erupts out of his mouth. I watch the life drain out of his eyes, and I feel something drain out of me, too. This is my first kill face to face, so much easier on the other side of a distant gun. Even the leader I fracked died while I ran away. But more than that, this seems like the first time I have looked into someone's eyes in a long, long time. I see myself reflected in his fading gaze. I look terrifying. What the hell have I become?

I leave my self-recrimination with the spear, buried in his chest like a marker and make my way into the motor pool. In the darkness, I collect my thoughts and calm down. I want to get this over with, I want to leave this evil territory forever, but I have no idea where we all can go and survive. I feel like I am in prison, like the fence I once snuck in and out through will close around me and trap me in this hell until I die.

"Could be sooner rather than later," I hear myself whisper. My subconscious, it seems, still has a sense of humor. I shake my head and resolve to finish the job. "Come on, girl, let's get this over with."

I shoulder my rifle and pick up two jerricans of gasoline. The weight is heavier than I expected, but I hustle back outside.

The crows are pecking at my fresh kill. They are working at the torn and broken flesh where my spear went in. They bounce back and forth from the bottom of the spear to the body, fighting for the narrow band of bloody flesh around the knife.

I ignore the crows and go back by the route I took when I fracked the leader. I make my way back up to the first level of the barracks, the gasoline waiting for me on the ground. I pull on the cords and they snake around the handle, then the cans follow me up the wall. On top, I pull the jerricans up and remove the caps.

I take down my rifle. I check all the guard towers. They are watching the fence, watching for an attack from the outside. Still, I make quick work of pouring the gasoline all over the roof, streams of fuel sliding down the outside walls.

When that is done, I grab my rifle and jump back down. I retrieve two more cans and douse the walls all around the barracks.

After my final circle around the barracks, I stalk back to my spear and murder of crows. They look up from their carrion and watch me walk past. I go back in the motor pool and thread three canisters of gasoline on a thick cord then drag them outside. I line the cans up near the barracks then open the caps and run back to my spear.

My heart beats in anticipation as pluck my spear out of the carrion. My crows squawk at me. They bounce off the ground and dance around me as I walk back toward the barracks.

"Do not fret, little birds, a bigger feast is coming your way," I tell them.

I take one canister of gas and go to the front door. I pour a hefty amount on the door then leave the can resting against the frame.

I walk around to back door then jam my spearpoint into the ground at an angle and press the butt of the spear against the door. Without ceremony, I find a shiny stream of gas on the wall and light it up.

The fire purrs as it rips across the building. I pick up an open jerrican then spin around multiple times to heave it onto the roof. A roar rolls across the base when the fire catches the opened can.

The Third Battle of the Base has started.

I grab the last canister of gasoline then heave it through a central window. I can hear yells from inside. Bullets are landing near me, pinging off the building, kicking up dirt. The guards in the towers are firing at me, but they are too far away to hit a moving target.

My rifle is poised in my hand as I make fast laps around the building. Soldiers try to escape out of the high windows, and I easily pick them off mid-climb. They slide back into the burning building, soon replaced by black plumes of smoke.

Guards are running up from the teenagers' barracks. I drop to a prone position, aim, and wait for them to come closer. They cannot see me with the fire and smoke swirling around. Overhead, my crows follow the barrel of my gun like a cavalry charge. I fire in quick succession. The guards drop, and my murder descends.

6

THE GUNS OF THE NORTH

~

My steps are cautious and light as I walk backward toward the motor pool, rifle up and aimed at the burning barracks. They are full of flames like stoked ovens baking their contents. Everyone inside must be dead. Anyone who could have survived the fire has exited, only to be picked off by my sure shot, so I keep my gun quick just in case.

The soldiers in the guard towers are still alive, still firing weak, faraway shots at me that do not get close to their target.

I need to take out those towers, but that is a problem. I cannot do it the way we did before, by driving up with the Humvees and filling them full of holes with the big machine-guns. I cannot operate the Humvee and big guns at the same time.

I look to the teenagers' barracks. I can see shapes of heads meekly looking out the window to view the battle I just fought. The heads poke up and retreat down at any gunshot or explosion. The teenagers are so beaten, so defeated that asking them for help with taking out the guard towers is not feasible.

Another option is to make peace. I could wave a white flag and approach, then trade mercy for safe passage. But walking up to a guard tower alone, asking for a truce sounds like a sure way to get shot. And knowing what I know about this decadent base and the soldiers who haunt it, even if they balked at shooting me, and I gave safe passage, stripped them of guns and let them go into the forest, as soon as they found the other soldiers out there and told them I was alone, they would come back to take me out.

Mercy is not safety. When I came to America, one of my first focused studies in my middle school social studies class was studying the American Civil War. As an Ethiopian, I was all too familiar with civil war—the most recent one wrecked my family, killed my uncles, and set us on a path of chaos that eventually led to our emigration to the United States.

Our history is so bloated with tales of wars and retribution that when I heard the full story of the American Civil War I was surprised by how weak it was, with no massacres of innocents, no famines, no decades-long struggle, no great acts of retribution. What astounded me most was not the war itself but the peace. What do you mean the Union did not line up all the Confederate rebels and shoot them dead? Ha. The guns of the North went silent? Odd. They won. It was their right, but more than anything, it was the safest course to take.

Later in the same class, I learned about the "great peace" and reconstruction which brought the KKK and Jim Crow laws and decades of systematic racism and violence. I felt vindicated in my view of the weakness of the North, felt vindicated, still, every time I saw a black teen shot by a white cop on the nightly news. The thought even spiked my intuition when Kevin told me about the government conspiracy regarding the caldera.

Mercy has its own risks. And maybe the guns of the North went silent too soon.

I will not be making peace with the soldiers in the guard towers. I reach the motor pool and slip in to grab another canister of gasoline. I tie it to the cords of my X and let it dangle heavy on my back. I pick up my rifle and head back out into the smoke-filled base.

Without hesitation, I sprint toward the closest guard tower with my gun raised, the gas canister bouncing off my butt like a war drum. The soldier finally sees me, but I juke, stop, then fire my gun while he is still trying to figure out the shadow running toward him. His head jerks back and explodes.

One down, three more to go. I turn left and head to the next one. My gunshot alerts the other towers, and I will not get lucky with an easy shot again. They are firing at me, but I am a hard target to hit. I start to fire back at the nearest tower. My shots are landing ne

ar the peephole, and the soldier finally ducks for cover. Big mistake. I sprint at the tower before he pops up again and find protection underneath the guardhouse above.

Nestled in safety directly beneath my target, I release the big canister of gasoline from my X, then pour a hefty amount on two of the heavy wooden posts holding up the tower. I quickly light the gas, and the ignited flames burn bright and crawl up the wood. The fire burns hot, but I keep my eyes and rifle pointed up the ladder to the hatch.

After a long wait, the flames are starting to die down, but the wood still burns, simmers, and cracks. I start to get impatient and doubt my plan. I take my water bottle and drink what is left. Then I fill it with gas and douse the flames

Finally, after much more burning, the posts finally weaken and buckle and the tower collapses to the ground while I skirt out of the way. Screaming comes from inside the broken and destroyed guardhouse. I tiptoe up to the rubble, poke my barrel in through a gap and follow the sound of the screams. I fire at the wailing and bring silence.

I can tell the soldier in the third tower is scared now. When he frantically fires at me running toward him, the shots are erratic and do not land close. The fourth tower is also frightened. He fires many faraway shots that have no chance at hitting me. I ignore him for now, take a minute to reload, and decide to directly attack the third tower.

After pinning him down with well-aimed shots, I go under the tower and put down my rifle. I climb the ladder with the gas canister hanging from my back. When I get to the top, I keep an eye on the hatch, but know it will not open because he was so timid on my approach. I place the half-empty gas canister on the top rung, then open the nozzle. I pull out my water bottle and pour a long stream of gasoline down the ladder. When I go back down, I feel for when the ladder becomes dry and light the gas above. Fire races up while I drop to the ground. The half-full canister explodes, and the tower is engulfed in flames.

As I run to toward the other tower, gunshots finally stop ringing out. "You are out of bullets, cowboy," I mutter to myself. In response, I see the hatch open, and the soldier desperately scales down the ladder. I shoot him when he hits the ground.

Behind me, I hear a yell and a thump as the other soldier jumps from the burning guardhouse. I turn back around. He is thrashing around on the ground, a heap of broken bones and bleeding skin, and the most merciful thing I have done today is to show no mercy.

CARRION CROWS

∿

They are all dead. I won. I really, really won.

Against the one percent odds I gave myself, I won the battle singlehandedly. I feel like a conquering hero. Behind me, as if pillars commemorating my victory—two guard towers smolder—one wrecked on the ground and one in the air burning like a limp tiki torch.

I pass the destroyed soldiers' barracks, pass by the courtyard and flagpole and head to the building where the enslaved teenagers live. I discard my stalking run and parade toward the barracks like a victor, like a conquering heroine returning home.

But there are no crowds waiting for me, no hurrahs and that-a-girls. The teenagers are still cowering in the barracks. I can hear shuffling and hushed voices. I can even smell their stench from outside—a disgusting reek of body odor and ketosis.

I gently rap on the door before slowly opening it. I was a bit disappointed in no welcoming party, but I am truly unprepared for what I see and smell. I take a step inside and the teenagers look at me with big, weak eyes set in skinny faces. They look starved and beaten down.

The smell of starvation hits me hard—the ketosis—an acrylic, plastic smell that comes when a starving body cannibalizes itself. My head is spinning, and I am back in Ethiopia. My mother, who grew up suffering in refugee camps in Somalia during the Ethiopian Civil War, took me and my brother to a camp of Somalians struggling to survive in Ethiopia. She felt it was her Christian duty, her Covenant of Mercy in Mary's name, to help the Muslims who once helped her when she was in Somalia. She also wanted my brother and me to know the specter of true suffering. Our lives were so protected up to that point and, I felt, she always wanted us to know what horrors could be around the corner.

For many Sundays we went through the camps, helping the aid organizations supply food and medicine, helping feed the new arrivals who came in like skeletons barely able to walk. I was always used to a plethora of smells in Ethiopia, but the smell of starvation carries an unnatural weight. Somehow, without food, humans start to smell like chemicals, acidic compounds used for a cleanse.

And this smell emanates from the teenagers. They are starving.

I focused so much on the killing that I forgot about the caring. I must grapple with the next part of the plan. I need to provide for them. I cannot take them to Caxm, so we need to make a home here. As much as that bothers me, it is our only choice.

"Hey, you are free. All the bad men are gone," I say.

I no longer expect my long-delayed hurrah, but they only look at me with pleading eyes.

"Food," one of them says.

"Yes, of course. Here, follow me." I turn around and start to lead them to the mess hall. Even though the teenagers have been starved, the soldiers looked healthy enough. There still must be food left; enough, I hope, until I can teach some of them how to hunt.

I turn around and walk backward to see the teenagers timidly leave their barracks. They seem shocked by the sun, shocked by the air, but they continue to follow me. I turn back around and head toward the mess hall.

Honestly, I am quite famished myself. I try to recall what meals were like on the base when we came here from Denver, when we still thought it was a refugee camp and not a colony. MREs and packaged food actually sounds good, maybe even something sweet, like chocolate. After a steady supply of venison, mutton, and nuts, chocolate would be nice.

I hear a collective moan from behind me. The teenagers have stopped walking and are looking at the burning building where the soldiers, their tormentors, slept.

Many of them are crying now, full of despair. Quite a few have collapsed to the ground.

Oh, no. Maybe some of the teenagers were sleeping with the enemy, for food, like Becky, Lily, and Kelly. If I burnt down the barracks, I killed them, too. And they were innocent, probably forced into sexual exploitation at gunpoint or via starvation, like the leader suggested before I killed him. And I hadn't even thought about it.

"You burned it down?" a tall boy asks. He is gaunt but still retains a tall, athletic frame.

"I am sorry. I…I forgot…were some of your friends sleeping with them?"

"You burned it all down!" he yells in desperation.

I feel terrible. I am no hero. I am just another killer of innocents.

"You burned all the food! They kept all the food with them!"

Everyone is yelling at me now. I feel scared. I take a couple of steps back even though I am the only one armed. They start running toward me, and I do not know what to do. They look like zombies from some terrible movie, emaciated and struggling to walk fast. They have dirty, lifeless faces that look past me with a great hunger.

A bunch of kids stagger right by me, and I realize I am not in danger. They are running to the smoldering barracks, to the last of the food supply I just burnt up.

I TURN and watch the surreal scene. In the background, the tower still burns like a darkened oracle, like the Eye of Sauron watching the depravity with delight. The teenagers prod and prick at the door of the barracks, scared of the fire. I caustically think that I will not be eating chocolate anytime soon when a girl covers her mouth with a tattered shirt and makes her way into the smoke-filled building.

Some boys follow her, and they rush back out, carrying charred boxes held in their smudged shirts. Between coughs and heaves, they start stacking the boxes and pick through the food, trying to see what is edible.

My mind starts spinning. The crows, the smoke, the hungry teenagers swirl into a chaotic mess of hellfire and brimstone. A crazy laugh escapes me. I cannot help but think it is comical. Have I become so cynical during my time in the forest hunting men that I think this is funny?

"Ha, Americans," the crows tell me. "With us, picking through burning remains for food."

I saw Somalis suffer and starve. I heard stories about Ethiopians, my family members even, starving and dying in our civil war. Am I so callous now that part of me thinks Americans scrounging for food is karma?

I remember when my brother came back at Christmas after his first semester at the University of Colorado. We gathered around the table with big eyes to hear his stories. We were so proud of him. I, too, was very proud even though I always competed with the unfair supremacy and attention he got for being a talented boy. I reveled in his stories of university, and imagined myself topping it by going to an Ivy League school and studying to be a doctor.

But when my family asked about the other students, about his friends and classmates, he got quiet. He finally said, "They have no idea how easy they have it. How lucky they are."

Everyone nodded in agreement. All Ethiopians at the table, we were fully aware of what the Americans were taking for granted.

But he went on. Not only did they take easy opportunity for granted, what bothered him most, what made him sad and introspective was the unfairness of it. "They succeed without even trying, without even caring. I worked—no, we worked—so hard, all of us worked so hard for me to get to this point. Some of us even died. And I will continue to have to work my ass — ah, butt off, but they will succeed no matter what, able to live off their parents' or grandparents' money, able to cruise into whatever career or non-career they want."

My brother was never so cynical, never so pensive, so his words hit hard. He was always brimming with confidence about his accomplishments, his grades, his track times, his beautiful girlfriends, that to see him feeling low and vulnerable shook me.

They succeed without even trying. How can I not feel some sense of smugness at American teenagers picking through burning debris for food? There are hunters who go out and make kills to survive, and there are scavengers that feed off the remains. America may have been a country of hunters once, but now they are like my carrion crows, living off the conquests and victories of the past.

Kevin once mentioned, in secret, that he thought the terrorists were not the ones behind the explosion that set off the super volcano. He heard and suspected it was our government. I pushed that crazy thought to the back of my mind. The military just made me a leader amongst leaders. They put such confidence in me that I suppressed what Kevin was saying. But now, watching the starving youth, maybe the people in the government, ghosts from a tainted, brutal past wanted to be hunters again. Maybe, that is why we were fighting halfway across the world, and why I have become a killer of men.

My murder mixes with the teenagers, trying to steal what food is salvageable. They take flight, squawking when swatted away, and part of me feels somewhat protective of my flock.

I start to walk toward the pile of burnt food and teenagers and crows but then stop in my tracks.

The tall teenage boy has dragged out a charred corpse. He skidded it out the door, ducking down, hunchbacked under the smoke like a sycophant bringing his master a sacrifice. At first, I think, he is right, we need to bury the dead, but I know he is too hungry to be concerned about such things.

He looks up at us and the crows as if looking for support and approval.

"What? They did it to us."

I am unsure what he means. No, I know what he means.

I see where this is going. I must stop it.

"Yes...." a corvid whisper emits, "Yes..."

"No! You are not doing that."

"Don't you know, AA-ron?" he pleads with me. His eyes look so crazy with the starvation and subjugation of the past few months that I do not recognize him. He stands up. I know him now. He is one of the boys who was in leadership training with me. The one who came up with my nickname, AA, then AA-ron. Which I thought stood for African American, but Kevin told me it meant affirmative action—a reference to his view of my unjustified placement—a black female, in leadership.

"Don't you know? They kept us alive as food or for fucks."

A flashback surges in my mind as I think of the *figure-Y* I saw in the courtyard on the night I fracked the leader. The victim was not a tortured Pax. It was food, a barbeque.

"I will bring you fresh food. Do not do that!"

But he just kneels back down and bites into the blackened, burnt flesh and tears it away with his teeth. And once more, I turn to escape. I run toward the forest with a frantic sense of urgency. I lift my legs as fast as I can as I try to keep the vomit down.

8

WHAT REMAINS

⁓

I feel naked, careless. I am hunting for deer with a desperation that goes against everything I have learned about hunting over the past few months. I have no camouflage. I pay no attention to the direction of the wind that could alert the deer to my scent. I run through the forest with reckless impatience. Sounds of breaking twigs, of scraping branches snap through the forest as I bumble around looking for any prey that easily avoids my commotion.

My crows have abandoned me. Their ka-kaws and symbiotic help has fled to a new master. They stayed back at the base, to feed on the pieces of destruction I left for them, to pick apart with the other scavengers.

This world is nothing but scavengers, scrounging around in the death and decay for a morsel of survival. Am I any different? Is hunting and killing any more noble than picking at the scraps. At least the scavengers do not create death. They just clean it up and move it along to the next stage.

"Stop," I tell myself. The teenagers I just freed need decent food, but I will provide nothing if I scare the prey away.

I take calming breaths. The battle I just fought single-handedly was so chaotic, was such a deadly rampage that I've forgotten how to hunt. Adrenaline wrecks my nerves and makes my muscles shake. I continue taking long, steady breaths to relax. I need stealth. I need to think like the deer. That is how I survived in the wilderness over the past few months. I learned the patterns of the herds, and the men for that matter, then knew where to wait.

Three days since I snuck into the base, and the last time I killed a deer was seven days before that. I was tracking three different herds, killing a deer every few weeks, not enough to spook them in a way that would change their behavior.

I close my eyes, but my head still moves back and forth as if to scan the scenery in my mind. Ten days is a long break to predict their current movement, but I listen to my intuition. She tells me where the closest herd should be grazing. I snap open my eyes and start my fast run to the edge of the river before the destruction of the forest fire. Trapped by the river and burnt forest, their territory is so limited that hunting them is no problem. My initial urgency was unwarranted. I know I will find deer there.

THE BEST WAY TO reach the herd is by heading to the burnt-out bridge Kevin destroyed and working my way up alongside the river though the undamaged part of the forest. But the fastest path to the bridge is through the fire-damaged trees, away from the road.

My worn shoes kick up clouds of ash and dirt as I run over the hills between scorched trees. I feel my heart rate increase as I pick up my pace. I am scared, exposed in this barren forest, without camouflage. The bright morning sun is highlighting me, casting long shadows easy to see. There is a chance that soldiers are still looking for me. I did not kill every single one; some had already left before I started my rampage. But I suspect they are long gone, safe on the other side of the river and over the cresting mountain.

Still, I feel exposed, targeted, like I am being watched. The feeling is so strong that I bolt behind a blackened stump to hide and scan my surroundings. My back presses against the tree, hiding me while I look in the direction from where I ran. My rifle is up, and I use the scope to repeat a slower more careful inspection.

I see no movement, no one tracking me, so I move a couple of feet away from the stump and start to assess the forest at my left side, somewhat shielded. Far off, barely visible through the scope, I see a human figure, prone like a sniper lying near a tree but covered in camouflage.

I focus the scope on the figure and wait for movement. I realize that I am not moving either, so this strategy may not be the best. Maybe I could fire my rifle into the body, just to be sure, but a gunshot may alert his friends.

After what seems like a long time, I feel OK with the prospect of being killed by someone who can out-wait me. Besides, I have a bunch of teenagers to feed and should avoid wasting time in a staring contest with a corpse.

I slowly rise to a crouched position. My rifle is still aimed at the prone figure. My stiff muscles complain as I make my way forward, still bent over and ready to fire or flee at any danger. I make my way closer then stop and reexamine through the scope.

There is no danger. The person is dead, but my heart is still pounding. My intuition, it seems, remains scared. I decide to throw caution to the wind for once and run toward the body.

I reach it and stare down. The skin is severely disfigured and burnt from the forest fire. Another charred body. The volcano is not the only thing releasing toxic ash. Still, why am I so scared of a cooked corpse? I literally have seen hundreds of burnt bodies, many even, since last night.

I cautiously walk around the body and examine it, without touching. The skull looks bashed in. The face is unrecognizable. The supplies have been scavenged. Many footsteps are pressed into the surrounding ash and dirt. No weapons or gear remain, until I see what looks like a small satchel protruding from underneath the body, and my heart starts to race. The initial fear I felt spikes up. I stare at the body and the bag underneath.

Finally, I take a step closer. With my foot, I nudge the body so I can pull out the bag. The bag is heavy and clunky for something not very big. I lift it up then grab the charred, bottom corner and flip the bag upside-down spilling out the contents.

Loud, blunt thumps come up from the ground through the plumes of ash. I start to feel nauseated. My head is spinning, and I want to throw-up. I bend over and look closer at the ground and the bag's contents. Dirty, but still shiny and unburnt, the glossy cell phones look so foreign in this blackened forest, almost like ancient artifacts from another time.

The truth of the useless relics kicks off a dry heave from my stomach. If I ate any food recently, I would surely vomit it out. I continue to stare at the cell phones through another round of gags and now I know for sure: I finally found Kevin.

I WANT to bury his body, but I can't stand to see him like this for another second. I run away. I bolt from the final truth I just found and the mixed-up feelings boiling inside of me. I used to worship Kevin. I was obsessed with his mind, his intelligence and sensitivity.

When I heard that he sold the girls into slavery and had this confirmed by Michael, I wrote him off, instantly. No man should treat girls that way. A man who abuses or facilitates the abuse of women is no man at all. All the admiration I had for him just vanished. But seeing him dead, with a bag of cell phones, brought back many confused feelings. I did not want him dead. I wanted him to explain to me, with his remarkable intelligence and foresight, why he thought the exploitation of women was OK.

I had that fake conversation many times with him, in my mind. I imagined him relating to some story of war and unrest in the Ethiopia before my birth to justify the way things are now. Selling the teenagers was a necessary choice to survive.

But survival is a choice and surviving in a world where we take do evil things to live builds a world not worth living in, for us and our progeny. A key to our evolution is not just to survive but leave the world survivable for our kids.

So, I keep running. I run away from Kevin and the duty to bury his body and run to where I hope the deer roam. I excuse my cowardice with the weak obligation to kill a deer and feed the teenagers.

The river flows against my run. Soot kicks up with my footsteps until I finally reach the green grass of a forest untouched by flame. I look down at my dirty feet and body, in contrast to the verdant, unburnt forest, and I remember that I am filthy.

I shed my costume and submerge my body into the cold, hard-flowing water of the river. There is blood, dirt, and grime covering my body. Three days ago, I snuck into the base unclean, and only got dirtier. Even before that, I do not recall the last time I dipped myself into the river and scrubbed myself clean. My need to scour myself of the stench of death and fire and ash is not some silly symbol; I need to de-scent, rid my body of the smell of human depravity that a herd of deer will be able to sense a mile away.

I sink deeper into the river, up to my shoulders, and feel it pull at me. I want to submerge completely below, let the cold water wash my face clean, but I fear if I go completely under I will let the river take me. The chill of this thought shocks me back to the task, to the strength of who I am, and I stand up. I climb up the muddy banks, shake off some water, and put my sundrenched camouflage back around me, basking in her heat.

An hour after I resume my run, I see movement in the distance and know I have found the herd. I do not even sneak around and snipe. I just break into my fast, quiet pace and run with my rifle in an aimed position. I keep running toward them until they hear something. One deer, then the others stop their grazing and look toward me. As soon as they look up, I stop, kneel, aim, and fire; one eye closes and the other looks through the scope at the biggest buck watching out for his herd.

9

BUCK

~

The deer bucks and jumps when my bullet blasts through its chest. The rest of the herd runs in the opposite direction without looking back, without concern for their fallen mate.

I copy their fast, frenetic pace. I need to get back to the base before things fall apart. I have spent too much time in the forest, seeing things that cannot be unseen.

With a new sense of urgency, I reach the dead deer. He is a big buck, plenty of venison to feed the teenagers. I take a quick, precautionary look around to make sure no other predators heard my gunshot. When all looks clear, I put down my rifle and unsheathe my knife.

I can make quick work of dressing the deer. Funny, I never hunted in my life before coming to Tajikistan. But thanks to my love for biology classes and my desire to one day be the first doctor in my family, I knew what I needed to do: remove the guts and drain the blood, just dissecting an animal—separating the pieces I do not want to eat from what I do.

But this meal is not for me or my tribe. This meal is for the teenagers I freed at the base. And they are near starvation. I plunge my knife into the anus and rip the torso upward, pulling my knife back, careful to avoid cutting the organs. This is the part that usually excites my crows, but they are not here. They are not dancing around the carcass waiting to feed on my discarded pieces.

It feels so strange without an audience, to do this part solely alone, that it piques my urgency, reminds me of why the crows did not follow me, why I need to hurry back to the base with food.

After the entrails are removed, I wipe my knife and hands in the long grass. There are still bits of blood and guts on my arms and hands, so I allow myself a quick break by heading toward the river.

I climb down the narrow bank and sink my arms up to the elbow in the mud. I use the wet clay to remove the bits of deer I could not remove in the grass. I rinse the mud off in the river and stare into the water, again.

Despite this, I still feel filthy. The call of the river and its cold oblivion pulls at me. I keep staring at the rushing water and want to fall in, to float away while being cleaned and leave everybody and everything behind. I shake my head. "This is not why you are here, Fetien," I tell myself. I snap out of my stupor and stand up, turning around to head back to the carcass and my rifle. I shake the water off my hands then unwrap a thick cord from across my body.

I weave the rope between the buck's antlers, neck, and snout, then wrap the remaining part around my shoulders. I pick up my rifle and begin to drag the heavy deer. A small stream of blood pours out as I move away from the river and back to the base.

Exhaustion overcomes me. I am close to the base, but my body is wrecked. I pulled the deer with all my might, hurrying to get back to the base, to prove to the ones I saved that I could be a savior, that I could provide for them. There is an ancient Chinese proverb about owing servitude to someone you save, and now, I fully understand this dilemma. I feel responsible for the teenagers. I remember their scorn when I saved them and they realized it was just me. There was no army, no humanitarians with food, supplies, and a route back home. Just a little black girl with a gun and a knack for killing.

I reach the hole under the fence and slip through. I turn around, gripping the rope and digging my heels into the dry soil. The fence digs into the buck's thick fur. I get the head and large antlers through, but the body is stuck. The hole is too small and I cannot push the deer back through the other side. I want to give up, just point the teenagers to the stuck buck and be on my way. But I will not leave this task unfinished. I must pay my dues; I must perform my one good deed.

I tie the antlers to the fence to lift the neck in an unnatural angle, then get out my knife and work at the ground. My knife breaks into the soil over and over as I stab it like some frantic killer. The dirt breaks into small clumps which I scoop away.

I continue this until my arms are weak and worn out. I clear about two cubic feet of dirt, then I release the buck's neck from the fence. I put my back into it and birth the deer through the fence. When it finally pops through, I fall to the ground.

Mid-day clouds slowly pass over me as I lay there. They shade the high-noon sun, and I want to fall asleep. I want to crawl into the hole I just expanded and pass out, wake up a new person on a new day.

But instead, I jump up and glance back at the base, hoping no one has spotted me. I look back down at the buck. Dirt and debris has collected in his fur. Despite the urgency, I kneel and desperately brush away the filth.

Dirt, mixed with blood and dried hard, breaks away from the fur and flies in my face. I use my knife to cut away the filth, scrubbing with the blade harder and harder until it looks clean, presentable, like I am offering a sacrifice to the gods. I stop my cleaning and run the cords back over my shoulders.

I look back to main barracks of the base. Smoke and small flames still lick around the destroyed building. The teenagers have carted out any food they think is edible. The boxes of food form a small, weak pile.

Was I too impatient? Was burning down the base the wrong decision? I did not see a better way, especially after they were alerted to my plan. Maybe, after all, my greatest mistake was doing it all by myself.

But I had no other choice. I continue my trek toward the main square. Far from the buildings, the fire did not touch the flagpole. The unflagged rope is still in place. The same rope that they attached to Michael, beaten down and chained up.

I try to avoid this thought while I hitch the cord I was using to drag the buck to the flagpole rope. Once fastened, I pull on the other side of the rope and hoist the deer off the ground and tie it off. I stare up the flagpole, to the clouds quickly making their way across the sky.

Is this what Michael saw? I start to feel queasy. I was away in the forest when Michael was whipped, but now I can imagine what he went through, the ordeal he felt when they tried to break him. Did they succeed? Did they break down Michael enough to make it OK for him to help Kevin sell the girls? And what did he mean in the temple when he yelled that we were not there? Was that meant for me? Should I give him a pass? He seemed so distraught, so broken when he confessed in the chapel. Is it enough for someone else to be broken, to allow them to be complicit in breaking other people? Hurt people hurt people, and all that.

I stare so long at the buck and the flagpole that when I snap out of it, I half expect to see a crowd of teenagers gathered around me with drooling mouths and eager faces at the feast I have brought them. But no one is there.

My walk to the teenagers is exhausted and clumsy. I make my way to the main barracks where the teenagers have gathered with my crows. They are hard to tell apart, bent over their meals and rummaging through the barracks, blackened with soot and hunger.

"Hey, I brought you a deer!" I yell.

They ignore me and continue with their scavenging.

"A deer! Look." I point back the way I came to the flagpole and my prize buck hanging from it.

"It's not cooked," one of the teenagers finally says to me. He looks up at me with a blank stare and dirty mouth.

"So, cook it," I start to say, but my voice only produces a whisper. I just stand there and revel in their ingratitude. A couple of other teenagers look up and nod with the entitled boy. They look down on me from their crouched, picking position.

They expect me to cook for them, I realize. They are worse than my carrion crows, who at least alert me to prey and eat my thrown-out offerings and thus pull their weight. There is no symbiotic relationship. There is just me, serving them.

I turn around and walk away, back to the motor pool that supplied all the gas I needed to burn down the soldiers. I open the door and look for a jeep that can carry me away from this evil base.

10

THIS IS THE END

~

Smoke still billows from the base, sauntering between burnt buildings and snuffed out bonfires like a haunting of ghosts. I look in the side view mirror and watch it swim in the changing breeze, caressing the ones I leave behind, surrounding them like an evil shroud.

Above them, my murder of crows circle—gliding through the smoke—excited about their feast. I take one last glance at the birds and the freed teenagers, then hit the gas. Maybe, that is why I chose the vehicle instead of my usual stealthy escape through the hole under the fence: I wanted a fast getaway so the scavengers could not follow. I wanted to be free from them feeding off me. Let them find their own way in the world.

I fired the jeep up and drove fast away from the base. It feels weird, surreal driving a vehicle after months of running through the forest. But I wanted a quick getaway and even my fleet feet could not take me away fast enough, away from the death, away from the depravity, away from the carrion crows living off both.

The big buck I killed for them hangs untouched, dangling

from the flagpole in the courtyard. My final payment made. My moral calculus for the ones I killed zeroed out by my saving the teenagers and pointing them to a path they ignored.

I barrel toward the exit. I am so eager to leave I do not stop to open the gate, just blast through it. My head jerks on impact. The jeep bucks but still splits apart the metal chains with a deafening din. I glance back through the remains of the gate and see the survivors glance at my exodus for a quick, pathetic second. They return to their scavenging, and I return my stare to the road ahead.

The drive is now accompanied by annoying noises from the front of the jeep. I should have stopped and opened the gate. But I press forward, driving over the hills and bumpy road until smoke from the base is no longer in my rear vision.

With the ash and smoke absent from the side view mirror, I stop the jeep, a bit sickened and unused to the smell and mechanical howl. In a need for clean, clear air I kill the engine. I stare at the steering wheel and absorb the silence.

Mentally, I pull a list together of what I have and what I am missing. The pistol rests on my hip. I was smart enough to grab a big tub of water, but I lack substantial food. My gaze goes down to my rifle riding shotgun. At least I can always use her to gather food. But the idea of hunting now repulses me.

I no longer have my camouflage. I gave the map to Charlotte and Lupina. I have no blankets, no way to camp at night. Caxm is compromised and no longer an option for me. I will never set foot on the base again, either. I am alone and unable to resupply.

"I am the only one now. I am the only one now." I repeat. I want to cry. My eyes well up. I have never felt so alone, which says a lot for a young, African immigrant. My teeth clench hard in my jaw as I shake my head, shake the weakness away. I look to the forest surrounding me.

My thoughts go to Lupina, Charlotte, and Jaden, alone on a mission to find Pax. I pointed a path to Charlotte on the map and sent them on a journey into a dangerous territory.

I finally come to the realization that *they* are my tribe. After the base selfishness I just witnessed, where people threw away their morals to survive. Or the treason of Eva; it's not the Tribe of Iodine Wine, not Caxm, not the teenagers I just left behind who weighed me down with the burden of responsibility. In many ways, more than my family, my home country, or my adopted country, I am tribeless except for those who are looking for Pax. That little gang is my tribe because they believe in goodness. They believe in love. In contrast to the cannibals I left behind, Lupina and her friends are sacrificing their safety to find the one who is trying to free the girls exploited by Kevin. And I must help them. This is my only path to redemption for the things I have done, for the person I have become.

I scan the forest again, looking for any danger. After lurking on the base for the past three days, spying and plotting against the decaying chaos of the remaining soldiers, the quiet forest is comforting.

I break the silence with a need to work, to move forward. Now that I have made my decision, I must take the necessary precautions. The place I am going to is even more dangerous than Tajikistan. No one is riding shotgun. No one is perched above me with a big machine-gun. If I hit trouble I must be able to escape into the forest carrying all my supplies in a few seconds.

"What supplies?" I laugh aloud, to no one. "Two guns, a knife, cord, a lighter, a bottle of rubbing alcohol, and a tub a water. What a fool." I shake my head at the self-deprecation. No! I am Fetien Mihirät. I am a survivor.

I take out my knife and jump into the backseat. I plunge the blade into the seat. The movement and motion feel familiar, comfortable. It satiates my anger and worry. But instead of blood and guts spilling out, the seat vomits soft, white foam. I discard it and continue my cutting.

Large swatches of vinyl start to pile up on the floorboard. I cut every scrap I can, even from the driver's seat. I jump out of the jeep and place the skinned seats on the hood of the jeep. A pathetic bounty of cloth, I wish I had Charlotte's help or at least my camouflage. I could go back to my nest and retrieve the costume, but no, there is no going back. I start poking small holes around the thick fabric.

The holes line up around the edges. I finish stabbing the fabric and start to string my cord through. I grab handfuls of stuffing from the seats and fill the vinyl panels on my chest. I tie the material tight across my torso. I wrap my legs and arms. When I finish, I grab my rifle and climb up on the hood. The fabric is too thin for the coming cold. With my next hunt, I will need to skin a deer and use the smoke-dried carcass for clothing. What a dazzling, *exotic* model I will make. Ha.

From the hood of the Humvee, I glance down into the jeep to look for anything else I can use. My reflection in the windshield surprises me, looks devilish, almost evil. Now, I know why Michael, big in his presence and guns looked so scared when he swiped away the fog and saw me towering above him. I startle at the sight of what looks like another person staring back at me from a weird angle. I do not recognize myself. My face is covered in smoky grime and blood. My tangled and wild hair still has leaves from my laurel woven into it, but my mane splashes out in a chaotic burst colored crimson by the setting sun. The new ensemble looks like something from a sci-fi movie, hardened and plastic dress and stance punctuated by the rifle and my hard, dirty stare.

I kneel and crawl closer to the glass, to see me. From behind, the sun casts a weird, orange glow reflected all around and burning bright in the windshield. I take a closer look at my face. I look into my eyes, set in a swirl of ash and blood, my once-bright eyes look like dim stars trying to breakthrough a shrouded night, like many of the night skies since the catastrophe blew toxic cinders into the sky.

My head starts to spin as I stare at myself. I have had so little human contact in the past few months that eye contact was a rarity. I am so foreign to myself because I forgot what it was like to connect to anyone.

And this woman staring back at me, this stranger...I remember coming to America and hearing so many comments about the way I looked. Some nice, some not, but just so often, so repeated that I developed a complex—no, more like a curiosity, ha, like the Americans—about my physical characteristics. I would lock myself in the bathroom and stare at myself for hours. Not out of vanity, more of an inquisitiveness about my features. Strong, Ethiopian features that I was used to seeing all my life but were such a novelty to Americans—black and white alike—but in different ways.

My thin nose, my "honey" skin, my big forehead that black American girls would like to point out. "Oh, you think you all that." My tall, skinny frame that they said they could break in half.

Or the white kids offering their many compliments which in time just turned out to be another way to split me off, to condescendingly identify me as something different.

And I am different. I am special. I realize as I look myself set in the light of the auburn bathed glass.

I also realize I have become what the military wanted me to become: a highly efficient killer of men. Kevin once told me that the military had a score for the survival effectiveness of every person in the world. Teenagers who were selected for the colonies had effective scores. The ones selected for leadership roles, like Cisco and me, had the top scores. Kevin said I had the highest rating of anyone in the leadership program, thus, higher than any teenager on the base. At the time, I felt confused by what he was telling me, overwhelmed at the foresight of the powerful American military and their belief in me to be more than just a shy, compliant girl. But now, after all we have been through, it turns out they were right. I have suffered enough to spread my suffering with ease.

I am no longer the girl hiding away in the bathroom, trying to grapple with the ordeal of being a curiosity. I am a woman, a queen. But with my stone hard gaze, my stain of smoke and blood, more than anything I am a killer of men. But I do not want to be that anymore. I want to choose love.

I jump down off the jeep and hop onto the eviscerated seat. I pick up some discarded, white foam and pull the rubbing alcohol out of my satchel. I pour a generous amount of the precious disinfectant on the foam. And I scrub my face hard. I wash away the blood, the months of forest dirt, and the hard, toxic ash from the caldera. My face stings at the cleansing. My eyes burn and my nostrils flare. I grab the rearview mirror and change the angle so I can see my face. The girl is still gone, but I feel clean.

"Hope," I breathe out.

I fire up the vehicle and drive down the road to find Lupina and Charlotte, to help them find the militia that bought our girls for a herd of sheep.

So, to find peace...I head to Afghanistan.

FIFTH STORY

PEACE PRIZE

Michael

MICHAEL

1

WAYPOINT

～

I shuffle through the trees heavy and unbalanced as the ammo boxes collide with low branches and swing back, knocking my ankles, scraping my shins, reminding me of the weight I must bear. Even though I am hurrying, my speed is too slow. I misjudged the weight of the guns and ammo. Worse than that, I underestimated the speed of Charlotte, Jaden, and Lupina.

Too confident in my manliness, too conceited about my gender and size, I figured I would have no trouble catching two girls, despite the weight hanging across my shoulders. The mountain crest looms in front of me, and I know if I don't catch them at the pass, with my weight and my fatigue, I will not be able to catch up on the downhill.

I feel a suffocating sense of desperation. After months of being alone, of being an outsider looking in, I no longer want solitude. Why was I so alone? Now, in my frantic attempt to crash through the forest, I think of this question. I literally had thousands of hours to myself in the Humvee and never contemplated it.

Maybe I didn't truly feel alone before. Maybe it was the

company of Anahita and her sweet, humming song. Maybe it was just being a part of Caxm. A stoic and useless guard was, at least, still something, a role, a part of the community. I watched over them for the return of the Red Wave...while Fetty did the real work of protection.

But now I feel so alone, so isolated, so useless, that I barrel through the brush, knocking down small trees, breaking off branches as I lumber toward the rocky crest. My eyes, beneath a furrowed brow dripping with sweat, keep a view on the rocks ahead, a waypoint for my bearings.

I push through the final stretch of trees, entering the outcropping of boulders. It feels surreal, surrounded by jutting and upright rocks like a worshipper in some ancient shrine, but I am still alone. Lupina, Charlotte, and Jaden are nowhere to be seen as I move through the megaliths looking for any sign of them.

"Guys? Guys?" I whisper through a shallow breath, too scared to raise my voice and show how vulnerable and desperate I am.

I stumble my way to a small rock sitting beneath a huge, protruding boulder that looks like a ship sinking. I shed my heavy rocket boxes, then place the machine gun to the side. I collapse on the rock shelf and bury my face in my hands. I have failed, even before I really started. My legs, strong and bulky from the squats, were useless on the hard, steep race up the mountain. I feel exhausted, ready to give up here and just lay beneath the robe Anahita gave me.

Tears start to come to my eyes. I never cried after I was whipped, or even when they came back for me in the night... I never cried, too defiant to break down, to let them win. I kept my tears buried deep. And they never surfaced, then or during all my alone time in the Humvee, but now I feel like I have lost all hope. I am completely alone.

I hide my eyes and wet cheeks underneath Anahita's robe. I cover my head like a boxer who has thrown in the towel. My elbows rest on my knees, and my head hangs under the cloth. I watch tears fall from the dark cover and hit the dirt beside my feet.

The tears seem foreign, out-of-body, like they aren't part of me, just an offering on a plate brought by ritual to a shrine.

Still breathing heavy from the climb, my heart drums loud in my ears. It plays a beat with the soft drops of tears. I start to laugh at this depressing, corny thought, like the old soul song, "Tears of a Clown" or whatever. I hear the beats get louder and louder and confusion covers me.

A quick, hard ding hits my shoulder. Something is wrong. I lift my head out of the spread-out robe and look around. I see no one, hear nothing until another beat hits the dirt. I look down and see a small pebble bounce and rest on the ground.

My head arches back and I look upside down, up the rock cliff. My eyes, still full of tears, spill out a new trail down the side of my face.

Above me, hovering above the crest of the big rock, I see Jaden, Charlotte, and Lupina's smiling faces. They are laying down, heads sticking out, so they can peer over the edge. The juxtaposition of them floating above me, in reverse, makes me dizzy.

"You OK, big guy?" Jaden asks.

"I am now," I say closing my eyes and widening my smile.

"Ah…that's the smile we've missed so much," Lupina says.

And I can't help but stretch the smile even more, cracking the frosted patina of evaporating tears.

"You wanna come up here? Or should we come down to you?" Jaden asks.

I stand up excited and ready to climb the steep cliff wall if needed. But I pause at the thought of tiring my legs out more, or truthfully, stepping away from my gun.

"Coming up," I say. I bend down to pick up the arsenal.

"Michael, leave it. We're safe," Lupina says.

"I got you covered," Jaden says through his boyish smile. He slips his rifle muzzle out over the edge in a weak show of strength.

"Ah, OK." I look up the cliff, unsure of the line.

"Dude, there's a path around back," Charlotte says.

"Or you can try the climb. Should be just a hop skip and a jump for you, big guy."

"I'll take the easy path." I start to walk around the big rock and throw nervous glances back at my dormant gun.

Lupina's short hair lifts and flutters awkward in the breeze, like a child learning to dance. A wide, curving expanse stretches out behind them. From a flat part near the apex of the rock, they all watch me hike up the steep ascent like they are sitting at a picnic —which they basically are. A map is spread out in front of them, weighed down with their food and water containers.

I make it to their picnic and try to catch my breath through my wide smile. My head feels light from heavy breathing.

"Whatsup?" I ask.

"You know, the usual. Just planning an impossible journey into Afghanistan to rescue the girls we sold for sheep to an armed militia."

"Oh, is that it?"

"And to save Pax so Lupina can finally get laid," Charlotte says.

"Mind if I join?"

"The getting laid part or the saving Pax part?" Jaden jokes.

"The only piece/peace I'm looking for is the one with doves and olive branches."

"We missed you." Lupina smiles. She comes over and gives me a big hug. I feel the sadness, the isolation of the past few months fall off me and roll back down the shipwreck boulder like a rockslide.

"Me too."

I let go and sit, settling near the edge, not fond of heights, but I want to be able to check on my guns and ammo. I keep one hand firm on the rock and turn to the group. Despite the absurdity of the situation, we're all smiles. The four of us, original theater friends, just missing Pax and Kevin. I know enough that if I bring that fact up we will all lose our smiles.

"So, what's the plan?" I ask.

"Well, before Fetty left, she gave us this map," Charlotte says. She kneels down in front of it, in a hunched, concentrated pose, familiar from so many hours bent over a needle and thread. Charlotte is so good at making connections, at stringing together a collection of fabric to make a garment, that she will lead us. She takes a quick glance at the map, while we are still trying to find our location, and she throws down waypoints, with quick spots on the terrain and topography.

"Day one." She points. "Day two, day three, by day six or so, we should be near the border."

I am still trying to figure out where we are now. Kevin told me the truth of our location, but the map covers so little territory that I can't center. The map misses any: "You are here" smiley face icons or dropped pins. Something seems off. I do see the base where we escaped from and that Charlotte's points skirt around it, but I still can't figure out our current location. Damn, and I won geography bees by staring at maps for hours.

"OK." We all acquiesce. If I can't even find where we are now, how can I argue about where we are going?

"We need to stay on the road to make that kind of time. So, let's be on our toes when we get there," she says while keeping a watchful eye on the base.

"I'll guard our rear," I offer but feel unsure of my recent delusions of importance—the grand protector—holed up in the Humvee while Fetty spent months in the wilderness killing our enemies on her own.

I eagerly want to ask about Fetty, if they know which way she went, if there is any chance she will rejoin us, but that would be another buzzkill. I nod as Charlotte continues.

"Fetty said she was tracking multiple tribes to avoid. The group that bought the girls and attacked the base came up from Afghanistan. We think they were probably fighting, harassing, and escaping the rogue American base near the border that now controls our former base in Tajikistan."

"What concerns me, though, is does Pax know this? Does he know they came up from Afghanistan?" Lupina says. "Just because Fetty knows they went south doesn't mean Pax tracked them there."

She looks up at me with her big, pleading eyes, wanting some insight into the war and Pax that would lead us to him. I try to think of Pax's capabilities, his fleet of foot, his logic, his rationale for going alone after those girls. All I can do is shrug.

"Pax could be anywhere," Charlotte says. "But if we track the tribe it's the best chance to find him. That was his goal. It should be ours, too."

Lupina stands up and steps closer to the edge. My fear of heights increases as she approaches the edge, amplified by my loss of control and the hopelessness of our mission to find Pax. At least I can keep myself from falling, but I can't keep her safe. I watch Lupina's face, looking for any sign of suicidal tendencies.

She looks content. She closes her eyes and extends her face into the breeze. Her budding bangs tickle her eyebrows.

I look back at Charlotte and Jaden, and they look calm but interested in what Lupina is doing, like a pack of wolves waiting for the leader to sniff out the direction of the hunt.

Lupina opens her eyes and scans the vista in front of us. To the left rests the valley with rows and rows of ordered trees, bountiful in their supply of fruits and nuts. A wide range of heirloom breeds that produce wonderful flavors not found in our factory farmed supermarkets back home. Nestled in the trees sit the yurts the tribe made. They look like alien orbs blooming in clouds of leaves. Beyond, framed by irrigation canals and new fields sits my Humvee shaded under an arch of branches. The vehicle hidden under the arch looks foreboding, like a dark cave I don't want to enter again.

To the right leads the road where we fought the last battle with the base from Afghanistan, where I stood tall and angry and exacted vengeance from behind the .50 caliber. It felt right, good, towering, and powerful as I dished out my revenge. I was so focused, so zoned in on our enemies, it felt almost mystical. I found my purpose—after all that happened to me—remove the bad men like divinely ordained punishment, but now I am not so sure. Maybe Fetty is right. Maybe, I too, am a bad man. But now, I just want to find peace.

Beyond the road, waves of forest roll into the mountains, stretching out over the cresting peaks. In the distance, beyond our sight, is the forest left bare by the fire that burned after Pax and Kevin disappeared, covering us once again in smoke and ash. Beyond that, far away, stand huge, towering mountains, rocky and lifeless.

Lupina looks at our path leading to the burned down forest and barren peaks. She turns to us with a soft smile. "Shall we begin?" We nod. She reaches out her hands. I stand up and take one then grasp Charlotte's as Jaden completes the connection. "No matter what happens, I am glad we are together."

2

STAR-CROSSED LOVERS

~

I n a delicate balance between food, supplies, time, and safety, we decided to walk the road south, a sacrifice of safety of the forest for a faster pace along a route with no branches and trees to encumber our hike.

Despite the heavy robe draped across my shoulders, the ropes carrying the ammo boxes have rubbed my skin raw. I clinch to the pain and know that the eventual callouses will make me tougher.

I bring up the rear with Lupina in front of me. Jaden, armed, leads with Charlotte right behind, pointing the way, doing the calculations between distance and time. We are not as self-sufficient as Fetty (or Pax, hopefully), and if we crawl along through the trees, we will run out of food too soon.

Speed is a crucial variable in the survival equation. Charlotte pushes us with a non-compromising demeanor. In her head she threads the calculations, and she is worried about our odds of surviving in the wilderness—let alone finding Pax and saving those girls.

We don't talk, except when needed. We just follow Charlotte, pushing Jaden to keep moving, keep walking. What makes the pace even more worrisome is that Charlotte is not some outdoorsy uber-hiker. She is naturally unimpressed with nature and not one to push herself physically. She throws looks at my guns and me if I start lagging too much because of the weight, as if, the weaponry offers more cost than benefit.

If she is pushing us hard now, she knows the odds of us surviving or at the very least finding Pax before we run out of food are low. I feel we all know this, not just Charlotte, but what is both more bothersome and beautiful is that we are still making the trek.

AFTER A LONG DAY, we are tired and sore. We follow Charlotte into the forest for the night. Far and yet near enough to the road, we set up camp, wordlessly gathering dead branches for the women to quickly weave into a lean-to.   e nights are colder but being huddled close together in their shelter should provide enough warmth.

"Fire?" Jaden asks, in contradiction to my optimistic thoughts about our shelter.

We all look at each like little kids who suggested a devious deed like searching porn or stealing candy.

"Can we?" Lupina asks Charlotte.

A huge part of the food/safety/time equation is not being discovered, but camaraderie is also key to our survival.

"A small one," she says. "And don't let it smolder."

I pick through the rejected branches, too small to lace into the lean-to, and make a tiny pyramid in a patch of earth Jaden scraped bare and ringed with small rocks. We place pine needles below and light it, but the F re doesn't take. Lupina comes over and pours a tiny amount of rubbing alcohol on the kindling and Jaden sets it aflame. Everyone stops working and just stares at the fire. I can tell others find comfort in this routine. The nightly fires of Caxm were a key part of their day, a capstone on on a hard day's work of building and surviving.

I watched these gatherings, with their stories and singing, alone, in my Humvee so much so that I still feel like an outsider, an interloper on a happiness and togetherness that I did not deserve. From a distance, I often wondered about what touching stories they would tell to bring about such warmth or laughter or suspense.

When the fire spreads its way around the small sticks, I start to add thicker branches. As if conditioned by the warmth Jaden, Charlotte, and Lupina automatically go into story mode.

"Michael, at story time the other night, we were talking about *Romeo and Julien*," Lupina says as if she knew I was wondering about their campꜰ re tales and wants to fold me into the tradition.

"Ha. Yeah, the Mexicans thought it was hilarious. They couldn't stop laughing at me," Jaden says. "And now I know a bunch of Spanish words for homosexual."

Charlotte gives him a loving, manhood-affirming squeeze.

"*Romeo and Julien*," I repeat. "Man, that seems like forever ago."

"*Maricón.*"

"But do you all remember Kevin's plan?" Lupina asks. "I've been thinking about it a lot lately."

"*Joto.*"

"We didn't follow it," Charlotte says.

"Yeah, we didn't follow it, but do you remember how crazy it was?"

"Wait, what did he want to do again?" Jaden asks.

"He wanted to mandatory-report the teacher, have Charlotte or I make some joking, casual comment about sexual assault, then later tell the administration that the teacher never reported it. He had it all worked out in his head. We would get the teacher fired so we could produce *Romeo and Julien*."

Charlotte seems nervous, a bit angered. She stares at the fire with her jaw clenched.

"And what did the teacher say when Michael tried out and nailed the audition for Romeo, and we all lobbied for him to get the part? 'But Romeo was Italian.'" Jaden says.

"Ha, yeah, that's what kicked off the firestorm. 'But Romeo was Italian.'"

"Like where we gonna find a fucking Italian to play Romeo?" Jaden says.

"I could have played an Italian Juliet, or Romeo, I guess." Charlotte adds. "If, you know, I wanted to be on stage. But you played it so much better anyway, sweetie." She looks at Jaden with an overwrought star-crossed lover smile.

When the teacher balked at a black male lead for Romeo, we took it up a notch and demanded Jaden play Juliet's part, too.

"I was surprised you ladies were cool with Michael and I playing both main parts, leaving nothing for the females."

"Well, we played most of the male roles in middle school, when you clowns were too immature and stupid to memorize a line."

"But what I've been thinking about the most, lately, is what Kevin was willing to do to win," Lupina says. We all stop talking to focus on her face, vivified in the firelight. "I mean, he was willing to get a teacher arrested and fake a sexual assault report just so we could have two black male leads in *Romeo and Juliet*. That's crazy," she tells the fire.

There is a long pause as we watch Lupina watching the fire. The light dances in her big eyes. "And Pax just went to the head of the theater department, pitched the idea of a modern adaptation about two black men in love whose families wouldn't let them marry and that was that, *Romeo and Julien*."

"And that was that."

THE DYING fire starts to smolder with coals, so we cover it in dirt. Charlotte wraps hot rocks in thick fabric and carries it over to the edges of our lean-to as a barrier of heat. Lupina joins her while Jaden and I piss on the fire to snuff it out.

The night air is already cold. We zip up, turn back around and see Charlotte and Lupina cuddled together in the middle of the lean-to. Our muscular, male bodies generate greater heat and more out of practicality than chivalry, Jaden and I will be near the outside openings of the lean-to.

Charlotte will be kept warm between Jaden's body and Lupina's. I feel an attraction to Lupina, of course; she is gorgeous, but I keep my distance and avoid the need to touch her. Aside from the distaste of betrayal, I feel infected, and I don't want it to spread to her.

I lay next to Lupina, but I don't touch her, for warmth or anything else. I hang part of my body outside the lean-to, embraced in the cold air.

Ironically, it took the timeless love story of Romeo and Juliet, played by two straight males, playing two gay characters, to wake me up to the pureness of love. An unadulterated purity that Romeo and Juliet/Julien felt for each other, that Fetty felt for Kevin, that Pax and Lupina share, that caused me to forswear the easy attention and lays of other girls.

After arriving in Tajikistan, despite all the chaos and worry about our plight, a part of me felt I had a chance to find a deep, forest love with Fetty, a fantasy constantly playing in my head. Part of me was even relieved when Kevin escaped over the fence. I thought I may even have had a chance to win Fetty over with Kevin gone, but every morning, before sunrise, Fetty would sneak out of our barracks and base to look for Kevin in the forest.

I was communicating with Kevin at the time, via his Bluetooth relay, and let him know when Fetty snuck out. He would keep his distance, hidden, while still keeping a protective guard over her.

Ironically, it was my love for Fetty that kicked off the killing. I saved her, then the Tribe saved me. And in the process, I sold girls into sexual slavery. Now, Fetty hates me. For good reason. In the frenzy of the violence I did something I should never have done — no matter what was done to me. I can admit that now. Fetty was right to attack me. And part of me feels I am to blame for the change in Fetty. Like maybe my selling of the girls and everything after spread the coldness and killer instinct to her. Or maybe that's just the kind of self-centered thought a brooding, Humvee dwelling person like me would think.

But no matter what, after all I did, I feel unlovable. I am patient zero on the Red Wave infection of our little tribe. I feel that no strong woman, Lupina, Fetty, or anyone would ever want to be with me. I take Anahita's thick felt robe and spread it across the women. I turn my back to nestled, sleeping Lupina and stare out into the forest as the cold air wheezes and stings, working its way through my broken nose.

3

COSMIC LOVE

~

W e travelled three days, unseen along the road, but our water is starting to run low. Soon we will be back at the bridge and the river where we can refill our water before crossing into the burned forest on the other side.

We crest a hill and the bridge comes into sight. An eerie feeling presses down on us, like we are being watched or chased again. The bridge was fixed enough to let vehicles pass, probably by the American-Afghani base that we fought before crossing months before. And now, the bridge and river would be a good choke-point to guard movement.

But we are eager to get water. We must balance this with the possibility that the bridge is a trap.

Staring at the crossing, I can't escape the feeling that the battle was only yesterday, and the symphony of gunfire will restart after a brief intermission.

"Let's fill up on water," Charlotte says with a voice dry and raspy. But nobody moves. We stare at the river and charred trees beyond.

Finally, Lupina walks past us all and heads toward the bridge. She turns around and walks back toward us while we still stare at the burned down forest. Without saying anything she just gathers our empty containers and heads to the river. Charlotte soon follows, which wakes Jaden from his daze. He jogs to the other side of the bridge and takes up guard. I follow his lead, but still feel like I am in a trance.

The feeling of continual combat should not be present; my heart shouldn't be racing. The battle was a long time ago, and we won. On the other side of the river, the traces of the clash: the bodies, the enemy Humvee that I took out, the blood and bullets, have all been removed or melted down back into the earth by the forest fire and other scroungers, but I have a strong vision, bordering on hallucina-tion, that the trees will sprout green again and push out the life that was extinguished, forcing us to fight again.

My eyesight starts to waiver. I stand at the foot of the bridge, unwilling to cross, unwilling to open the door back into the battle and the scorched forest. I see shards of light from the corners of my vision that seem to seep in closer to the center. I nervously massage the trigger guard of my gun ready to fire back into the forest at the reanimated bodies I put down. In a stupor, I cross the bridge toward the ash and decay of the forest felled by fire.

Up the hill, skeletal trees stand, looking like grave markers, weird, decadent crucifixes left bare by the forest fire when we burned the bridge to cover our escape. The fire spread and destroyed the forest on the other side of the river.

"Michael, Michael!" I hear a far-off yell from behind, loud but drowned out by the flowing water.

I turn around to see Jaden, Lupina, and Charlotte in a semi-circle, fifty feet away from the bridge. I thought the girls were still filling up water, but by the looks on their faces, I get the impres-sion that they have been yelling at me for a while. How long was I staring at the other side of the bridge?

Lupina waves me over. I walk back across the bridge toward

them; my heavy weight clomping down on the wooden boards hastily fixed across the beams. I turn back once more toward the burned down forest to make sure no corpses are following me across.

I make it to my friends.

"Are you OK?" Lupina asks and they all look up to me with concerned looks.

"Man, you look like you saw a ghost."

I am wordless, can only shake my head.

"Sam was buried here. In our hurry to escape the base, we never said words for him. I poured some drops of iodine, but we never said anything."

"OK." I complete the circle around the grave.

Lupina begins. "We don't know what happens when we die. We're not supposed to know. We have beliefs in gods, in heavens, and other things that make for comfort, but we live and die in a twilight of uncertainty.

"Sam, we don't know what has become of you, but we miss you. We miss your sandy hair and wide smile and the way you would bounce over any obstacle. We miss that cosmic connection you had with your brother. We named our village for you. Your name, pronounced in Tajiki, means share. I like that.

"I like to think to that if there is a known in the beyond, that you are watching over us, sharing your protection with your brother and your namesake village. Please watch over them while we are gone. They need your bouncing heart."

Lupina wipes her tears and dribbles them over the uneven ground of his unmarked grave and walks away back toward the road, the bridge, and the charred forest.

"I need your bouncing heart," I whisper to the grave and the buried bodies deep in the unknown and turn to follow Lupina across the bridge.

But now she stops. She tenses up and her gaze goes up past the bridge, to the road and the burned forest and I wonder if she is feeling what I felt, the uneasy feeling of one long, continuous battle we will never stop fighting.

Then I hear it, too. A soft, growing growl coming our way. This is not a dream — something is coming. I run to her side to be useful, to be a protector. Lupina takes a deep breath.

"Choose love," I hear her say. Then she starts walking again, alone, across the bridge, toward the growing rumble.

Am I hearing things? I wonder because of Lupina's brave walk forward, that maybe there isn't a rumble coming our way, just another ghost. I glance at Jaden.

He looks scared, too. He shakes his head and calls after Lupina, still crossing the bridge.

"Stop!" We yell at her.

The sound of the vehicle is building louder and louder. It will crest the hill on the other side at any moment but Lupina keeps walking toward it.

Lupina is too far for me to stop now; the best way for me to protect her is to set up my gun and get ready to fire at the approaching sound, our first contact since being on the old jeep road. I drop the rocket boxes and place the muzzle on the guard rail of the bridge as Jaden feeds a belt of ammo into it.

Memories of our last battle coming flashing across my vision. I try to recall how I took out that lead vehicle, when it came flying around a bend to be surprised by our waiting watch. I just focused on the steering wheel and filled the driver with two bursts then worked on the gunner as their Humvee crashed.

I cock the .50 caliber and put my finger on the trigger as the vehicle comes over the crest. I want to fire, but Lupina is in the path of the Humvee. If I shoot the driver, the vehicle may lose control and crash into Lupina. I move my aim to the turret, but it is empty.

Charlotte notices the same thing and yells at me.

"Hold your fire! Hold your fire!"

"Fetty."

4

A TRAVELER FROM AN ANTIQUE LAND

~

"**S**am saved us."

"What's that?"

"If Lupina didn't call me back, I would have crossed the bridge to the burned forest, gone up the road and been surprised by Fetty. Alone, near the last battle, all messed up thinking about the killing, I would have probably fired on her between the charred trees. He saved us. You know, maybe he is really watching over us."

"She saved us," Charlotte says with a nod toward Lupina. "If she didn't keep us all together, if she didn't call you back for the eulogy, then you would have been up the road firing at whatever stupid ghost you thought was driving the Humvee."

"Well, yeah, but still."

Charlotte gives me a look, then walks toward the Humvee as Fetty jumps down with a big smile aimed at the girls. She looks surreal, wearing patches of vinyl amour sewn together and stuffed with white foam. Down her back hangs a deer skin still shiny in the black and red of smoke-dried blood. The carcass cape is fastened around her shoulders to the top part of the deer skull which rest on her sternum, atop her foam padded vinyl cloth. The smallish antlers hang down and wrap her ribs, webbed together with cord. The muzzle of her rifle rests across her adorned shoulders and is held tight in Fetty's hand. Her face is wiped clean and shiny, but bright eyes still show a hardened, deadly edge.

"Girl, what are you wearing?" Jaden says.

"Love it, love it, love it!" Charlotte adds with uncharacteristic enthusiasm.

They are all smiles, happy at the reunion, looking at each other, and taking in Fetty's sci-fi outfit. I slowly approach, keenly aware that different timing would have resulted in me shooting Fetty, spreading my infection in the worst possible way. She already hates me, and now, being a danger, I feel even more useless.

As if picking up on my timid encroachment and outsider status, Fetty loses her smile and glares at me. The bridge of my nose starts to throb.

"What is he doing here?" she asks.

I want to defend myself but have no words, no position that could convince her to forgive me.

"Fetty, it's OK," Lupina says, and I feel great relief that she is my advocate.

"No, it's not. You know what he did, right?"

"He wants to help."

I feel like a child whose parents are arguing over him while ignoring him, another badge of uselessness.

"*He wants to help?* Just curious — so it was OK for Pax to kill Kevin, to issue a self-executed death sentence over what they did, but you just automatically forgive Michael?"

"Ha, yeah, the white guilt runs strong with these two," Jaden says with a half-laugh to break the tension.

I throw a scold toward my *brother,* Jaden. He should know better. As if me being black offers some kind of special status, some easy forgiveness that goes against high incarceration rates, police brutality, and everything else we learned as black boys growing up in America. I want to jump into the conversation; I start to form my argument attacking Jaden's hypocrisy, but then I realize he is right.

There are only two kinds of white people, those who patronize us—give us a pass and pats on the back and warm, bias confirming comfort when we fail. A look that says they're on our side when they let shit slide. They seek us out in a crowd of white people and awkwardly point out that 'Black Lives Matter' or 'I'm not racist.' In many ways, it's as bad as being sought out in a crowd and told 'All Lives Matter.'

And those white people, the 'All Lives Matter' ones, are unable to see it's not an either/or situation. Or worse, not caring, a thinly veiled lie that only white lives matter, and they are counting backward to zero. What did Kevin once tell me? "The criminal justice system promotes eugenics," lock them black boys up so they can't reproduce or better yet, put them in the ground. Either way, they know our place.

"Michael is not forgiven," Lupina says. "He is on this road looking for the same thing you are, Fetien."

Fetty eyes narrow, and her cold, questioning stare is back and focused on Lupina.

"Redemption."

"Whatever," Fetty says and turns to me with her fierce look; god, she is intimidating. "You're riding on top of the jeep, in the turret. I don't want to be near you."

"No problem. I know my place…back of the bus."

She steps toward me and my heart starts to race.

"Do not start! You have no right to claim the victim after what you did. Ever."

THE WIND FEELS good on my dirty, grime-laden face. The gun snugs firm in its bracket on the turret. My shoulders feel strong, proud, towering above all with no ammo boxes strapped across my shoulders; they too, are in position, fed into the gun and ready to strike. Exile suits me. Despite my shame and banishment and condemnation by Fetty, I feel powerful, comfortable, in the right place, back at the turret, a king on his throne, with the formidable Fetty driving the Humvee. We are an odd and at-odds couple but a powerful duo nonetheless. And I feel more confident in our crazy mission now that we are all together.

Jaden is riding shotgun, rifle nearby, while Charlotte and Lupina sit on the flayed seats leaking their whiteness in the back. We are making great time, so much faster than our previous trek by foot, which seems weak and inconsequential in comparison. I hear words flutter out the window but pay no attention. We are on the road, on our mission.

After being cast back to the turret, the other four discussed our plan while I set up the gun and watched the road. Fetty spread the re-appropriated map across the hood while others gathered around. I was ignored and left with fastening my toys to the turret.

Fetty traced the road down off the map to draw a line through the dust and ash on the hood. She drew a bigger line perpendicular with her flattened thumb then dotted the intersection.

"Starting in Badakhshan, I think this road eventually leads to the Pamir Highway, near Afghanistan. Before we cross that highway, we need to hide the Humvee, so don't get too comfortable with the ride, but this should save us a few days of hiking."

Curious, to know how Fetty knew we would have been on the road, Charlotte, the master of our itinerary, asked, "Did you go to the base?"

She nodded her head but didn't say anything. I stopped working on the turret and looked at Fetty. She is wrong about our location, but I feel too defeated to say anything.

"So, you came back up the road to look for us. Or were you heading to Caxm?" Charlotte kept pressing

"Not Caxm. I was looking for you." She looked sad like she wanted to say more but didn't know how.

"How did you know we would be on the road and not in the forest?"

Fetty's look was burned into me as I stood at the turret, weapon in hand, with delusions of power. She looked at each one of us like a parent to their children, and never have I felt so small.

"You are not people of the forest. You are babes in the wood."

"And Pax, is he a people of the forest?"

"Well, he is by now, or he is dead."

"Ha," I laughed. Tired of being looked down on, from high-atop the turret, I wanted to yell out, a loud he-haw into the air, maybe accentuated by the quick blast into the sky by the .50 caliber. A reminder that I, too, have killed people. Hat I am ready for the Red Wave. Hell, even shy Charlotte slit a man's throat to start the killing game. I want to defend my manliness against the little girl I love who broke my nose, to prove that I am worthy, but I only let out a teenager's snicker.

They all, even Lupina, gave me a disgusted look, confirming my exile. I was laughing at Fetty's incorrect analogy, not Pax being dead.

"They are not people of the forest," I said, to clarify my rude chuckle. "They are people of the desert, and we are not where you think we are."

Fetty and Charlotte cocked their heads and threw me a look exposing my vague bullshit statement being used to work my way back in their conversation and good graces.

"And…where are we?" Charlotte sardonically asked.

"The map Kevin gave you is a small one, only covering the area around the base. Caxm isn't on it, and neither is where we are going."

"No shit."

"In his big speech about the grisly beginning and the mountain, Kevin told us we were going to Badakhshan, but that was a lie."

"Why?"

I stood up taller from the turret like a pastor preaching the truth. They still just stared at me with doubting looks.

"He knew there were spies in our camp, or tribe, so he gave a false destination, knowing it would leak back to the other teenagers and eventually the rebelling soldiers and throw them off our trail."

"So."

"So, we didn't go to Badakhshan. Caxm is farther north. And the way to Afghanistan is a long grueling one through a mountainous desert, through Badakhshan. In other words, we are starting farther away than you think."

Fetty stared at me for a long time not saying anything. I thought, or hoped, that my information was useful, was a worthy gift to begin forgiveness. But she wasn't considering absolution; her mind was elsewhere. She dismissed me with a look and turned back to Charlotte, Jaden, and Lupina.

"Before I fracked the other leader, he told me that Kevin called their base on the radio, right after we killed all the soldiers. He taunted the other base, challenged them to come up and stop us, said something about a counting coup with death."

Lupina's jaw dropped at the crazy news of Kevin's challenge, but Jaden and I scoff. Ha, counting coup, we know the story the leader told is true. In Denver, Kevin copied the Native American game of going up to your mortal enemy and tapping them on the shoulder with a coup stick, then escape away before they could do you harm. Although, the enemy Kevin was always going after was death.

"I thought about that a lot after I killed the racist leader. Why would Kevin do such a thing? But then I realized, he was timing the American-Afghani attack of our base to hit while the militia occupied it. He was pitting them against each other."

"So, he was an evil genius. I think we all pretty much figured that out by now," Jaden said.

"Yeah, but let's remember the timing. It took the other base, going all out in their vehicles over rough jeep roads, two days to reach us."

"Ah, so, they are probably around two to three hundred miles away," Charlotte says.

"By jeep then?"

"Until we reach the border."

"Or run out of gas."

"Or get attacked."

5

UNADULTERATED

◈

The felt robe that Anahita gave me is cut to pieces. Days ago, Charlotte took her big scissors, shrugged out a weak promise of being able to stitch it all back together, then cut away.

We wear the long pieces of felt like turbans to protect our head and faces from the high heat and unrelenting sun. Dirty swatches of cloth that we frequently unravel then dip into the rapid river we are following, swollen with glacial water, to be wrapped back onto our heads, dripping cold salvation.

We travel mainly around twilight, spurned by frigid nights to start our crawling across the stony terrain, cutting our hands and shins in the waning moonlight. We keep pushing through dawn until the risen sun is too much to bear, then we look for a cave or dig a siesta shelter under big boulders and wet strips of Anahita's robe.

If we are lucky, meat we have hunted cooks in the sun from which we are hiding. Strips of flesh cut thin and laid out on rocks under Lupina's solar oven. We salvaged the Humvee; hid it with half a tank of gas, then took or made tools from it. The bare-bones vehicle can still run if we ever make it back, with enough gas, I hope, to take us back to Caxm and Anahita's sweet song, hot tea, and dried fruit. But at least now we have more supplies to survive the rocky, high-desert of Badakhshan.

Jaden carries an axe and small shovel crossed over his back and fastened with Fetty's rope. Charlotte is armed with a compression slingshot made from springs and metal stripped from the already eviscerated seats. The slingshot can launch small rocks well over 100 mph, bursting small animals in clouds of fur or feathers, and saving us from wasting bullets or firing a loud report in the stone canyons. Honestly, with my size and the weight I must carry, I am consuming the same number of calories as the rest of the group combined and another heavy debt I owe Charlotte is that half of her hunting goes to maintaining my diet.

Like the rock-rocket launcher, Lupina's solar oven—concentrating light from multiple small windows—has proven critical. The oven allows us to dry the meat without a fire which we couldn't make even if we wanted to chance the smoke. Our route offers few trees or much vegetation as if the sun has already burned up anything combustible, leaving only stone and a cold river cutting its way through the hard land.

I still just carry my arsenal, strapped across my shoulders with rope and padded with more felt strips. I am faster now; my legs have a rock-hard feel that matches the terrain, but I still lag behind the others, especially Fetty who scouts ahead and behind like the shepherd dogs that guard Annie and Paco's herd. She is running two to three times our distance and is always ready to move on.

After more days than I can keep track of, she comes back to us with eager news. We sit on the bank of the river and wash the dried flesh down with silty water. We've lost all manners when it comes worrying about whether Fetty needs food breaks. She is an extraordinary machine and totally self-sufficient. And besides, we haven't seen her since the night before.

Without a sound, she appears on large boulder behind us.

"Good news, bad news," she says.

We turn and hold our calloused hands against damp turbans, more to block the sun than salute our savior. No one says anything.

"So, I found the road and the border. We are near Afghanistan."

"Is that the good news or bad news?" Jaden asks.

"Good," she says without humor.

"Great, can't wait for the bad."

"There's a huge river that marks the border. We will need to cross it."

Everyone turns back to the river and our snacks. We just stare at the water and contemplate what that means. We are all too familiar with rivers and bridges and the chokepoints they bring.

"Is the bridge guarded?" I ask, looking to my dormant gun.

"I ran several miles downriver. And I never saw a bridge."

We all turn back around and gape at her.

AT DUSK we make it to the river. I feel a pit in my stomach, a premonition of loss as I gaze at the wide waterway and know I can't get my gun and ammo across. I sense a smugness from the others at the irony of this, an internal laugh and Chekov eye-roll; I lugged my gun hundreds of miles to lose it to a dirty river.

We stand there for a long time, staring at the immense river, an impossible crossing with any extra weight, let alone my heavy ordinance. We watch the flowing river, so mesmerized that we don't sense someone else sneak up from behind, down from the stark, lifeless mountain we ignored. Another surprise, but this time, even Fetty is caught off guard.

"Lupina?" a raspy voice asks.

At the same time, we are instantly startled by the odd voice and eased by the name whispered. We know we are safe. We have found Pax, or better yet, Pax has found us.

There are no yells, no callouts. We turn and take Pax in.

He is almost unrecognizable. His piercing grey eyes shine in a face darkened with grit, a virile tan and facial hair giving him a look well-beyond his years. His long hair has dreaded. He wears clothes and shoes patched together with animal fur and looks primitive and striking, both in handsomeness and danger. He carries Fetty's formidableness and her prediction: he is a people of the forest; he survived, but he is not alone.

Lily, one of the girls we traded—no, one of the girls I am responsible for selling into slavery—is next to him. She looks different, too, almost more stunning without make-up and pretensions. Her hair is slicked back with grease and matted. Her tan face and mane look leonine, more so with a new hardness and clenched jaw. She stares me down through cinched eyes like a huntress focusing on a kill.

They stand on the rocks, together, looking down on us like a primal couple, like cave dwellers who are the genesis of a people. I start to worry about Lupina. Has she been pining for a love that has moved on? Maybe I should have wrapped my arms around her in the night instead of my robe.

We all look at each other and don't know what to say. I move my gaze to Lupina, but she just stares at him with a loving longing.

Finally, Jaden breaks the silence. "Damn, Pax, dreads. Fucking dreads. First the sneakers then the rap music and swagger, and now you take our haircut. Cultural appropriation is a bitch, bitch."

"I'm sorry," he says. But he is looking straight at Lupina. "I shouldn't have left. I should have communicated with you. I should have told you what was going on…with me, with Kevin, and with the tribe. I was wrong."

He hops down off the boulders and nimbly maneuvers to face Lupina. He cups her cheek in his hand, and she does the same. We all watch them stare into each other's eyes. After a long time of hardness, it is a sweet dessert in a bitter, dry land.

"I felt ashamed, of who I was as a person, of not stopping Kevin. I felt unworthy of your love until I saved the girls."

Lupina only shakes her head while staring up at him. Pax finally turns to us.

"I have a cave," he nods up the mountain behind us. "I have been scoping the river. I found a way across. First, though, we need some privacy. May I?"

He offers his hand to Lupina. She nods and whispers, "Finally." He takes her hand then guides her over the rocks and back up the mountain to his hidden cave.

"We need to debrief the situation," Fetty says.

"Later," he says without turning back toward us.

And to this we have no reply, not even Jaden.

6

SURE SHOT

～

W e are left alone with no answers and Lily and the
confluence of two rivers—the one we have been
following and the one we must cross—they bleed
together as the cold, blue glacial water from our rapid river blends
into the brown silt of the larger one, the Panj, then disappears into
the dirty, flowing sediment.

Jaden has taken to skipping rocks into the wide, slow Panj.
When the rock's momentum starts to wane, and the final skip
brings a stunted sink into the river, Charlotte launches a missile
out of her slingshot, trying to hit the slowing stone before it goes
under. She gets remarkably close to the target.

I watch Jaden and Charlotte's skeet shooting game, trying to
avoid the awkwardness of those left out of the cave to the weird
mood on the rocks. Between the obvious sex going on in the cave
and the impossibility of me apologizing to Lily, a heavy silence
hangs in the air, interrupted only by the splashes of Jaden's rocks
and the clang and burst from Charlotte's slingshot.

I feel a need to be defensive, not just to the hate-stares from

Lily, but the judgement from everyone. *Well, your people probably sold my people, so now we're even. Sorry, dude, about the enslavement.* There is really no way to apologize for what I did.

Normally so calm and calculating, Fetty seems agitated, and I wonder if seeing Lily is bringing up thoughts of her own near rape —that I stopped—hey, is that a legitimate defense of my crime? *You win some, you lose some.*

A loud ping comes from the river as Charlotte finally nails one of Jaden's rocks in mid-skip. She looks towards us with a dangerous smile.

Fetty pays her sure shot no mind. She paces back and forth on the rocks while massaging the stock of her rifle like a touchstone, looking between Lily and me.

She finally turns to Lily and asks, "Did he touch you?"

Charlotte, too, stops slinging stones and leans in for the answer.

"Pax?" Lily asks.

Fetty and Charlotte nod.

"No. He's been nothing but a gentleman." With this she looks at me, and I can't help but feel shame.

"No one has touched me. No one owns me," she continues.

"What happened? We heard you were sold to a tribe," Fetty says, cutting right to the point.

Lily seems angered by the question. I look her over for any weapons, any way to strike out at me, but she is only armed with a knife. Still, I feel threatened under Fetty's worn gun and Charlotte's lethal slingshot.

"We weren't sold. We were discarded."

"I thought Kevin, Michael, and Eva traded you for sheep."

"Ha. Is that what you think? Figures. No, he traded the base for the sheep. Kevin made a deal with the locals and the Afghani bands fighting the American Army, that if he destroyed the base they would give him a herd of sheep and safe passage."

"So why did he, why did we...I, escort you to the tribe," I say, flustered.

"*Escort me?* Hmmm, not sure I would call being tied up, dragged, and discarded an escort. But we weren't sold, Kevin just wanted to punish us."

It fits. Kevin seems to have a penchant for over-revenge: Danny's knee, the police department who harassed Jaden and I, the base and the girls. I wonder if his payback makes what I did better or worse.

WHEN THE AWKWARD conversation and the rock-skeet-sling game tires, we find shelter in between the boulders. Jaden and Charlotte, inspired by our reunited friends, sneak off to a large outcropping of megaliths downriver. Fetty remains on guard while Lily and I go off in opposite directions.

There is no movement, no sound except the rivers and the pacing of Fetty's fealty guard over the lost kids scattered among the boulders of Badakhshan. I feel naked, exposed, surrounded by animosity with my only ally, Lupina, away in a cave with Pax.

I can't sleep, can't gain the needed rest in our daily siestas. I just stare at the confluence of rivers while feeling sorry for myself, feeling the guilt of all I've done pile up inside of me and weigh me down. Part of me wants to discard the shame and ostracization I feel. Wash myself in the cleansing waters of the Red Wave and just write off any crimes to survival of the fittest. In many ways, that is the only law now and the only crime is to lose to it.

Later, I am awakened from my self-deprecation and deep stares by smiles. With no sound, I know they are behind me. Everyone else must know, too, as Jaden, Charlotte, Lily, and Fetty all congregate when Pax and Lupina appear on the rocks below the mountain.

They hold each other's hands tight, like champions. Their smiles, too, shine in merriment like they are ready to receive winning medals after years of training. We expect them to raise their clasped hands in victory.

Fetty, though, is unimpressed. "We need to talk. I need to know what is going on."

Pax shrugs and turns around with Lupina and heads back toward the cave. We stand still, wondering what this means.

"Round two?" Jaden mumbles.

But Pax stops and throws over his shoulder, "Come on. We can talk in the cave. It's safer."

THE CAVE IS dark and cozy, the size of a living room back home. A couple of goat pelts are spread out on the floor by the foot of a stove made from rocks and discarded metal. A small pile of branches and dung sits next to the ire. Skewers of dried meat wrapped in local herbs hang above the coals. Pax grabs a pair and hands them out like a refined host.

"I poached a couple of goats, kids that wandered off from their herd."

Hungry, Jaden and I take the skewers and relish the deeper flavor, different than the sun-dried small game and birds Charlotte has been picking off.

"What do you want to know?" Pax asks Fetty.

Fetty stands at the foot of the cave, sunlight basking around her, silhouetting her body and rifle in a strange halo The weak light from the fire shines on her vinyl amour and highlights the strong angles of her face. She looks dark, brooding, even more formidable than usual and all of a sudden, I feel sad for her, sad for the person she was forced to become, sad, I guess, for all the people we were forced to become since the Red Wave crashed back over us. Pax is a murderer. Kevin is dead. I, too, am a ghost in some kind of purgatory between bloodied revenge and self-banishment.

"First off, I want to know where you were the night the professional soldiers were murdered by the National Guard. Second, I want to know where you disappeared to when I was leading our group in the Battle of the Base. And finally, what the hell did you do to Kevin? Did you kill him?"

Her words are strong, shocking, like a dip in the river. Everyone tenses up, especially Lupina, but Pax just nibbles on some goat meat.

"Pax was with me the night the soldiers died, Fetty," Lupina says. "We fell asleep on the roof of the barracks, slept between the pine branches until sunrise. You could have asked me that at any time over the last couple of weeks."

Fetty and Pax don't say anything, just stare at each other. I see a smirk coming from Pax as he chews the meat.

"The night the soldiers died," Lily speaks up and everyone but Pax focuses on her. He keeps watching Fetty between bites as the women defend him. "Pax came to see if the corporal was dead. After he killed him," she says, pointing at me, "Kevin jailed us under Eva's guard in his room. Pax pushed open the door, to see the corporal dead, stabbed through the heart, and laying in a pool of blood. We were terrified, huddled together in the corner, when Pax looked inside, but he was different then, too, a scared and unsure boy, and he ran away. But that's why Pax killed Kevin, because of what he did to us, throwing us away like we were garbage." On the last sentence she stares at me, and I feel both remorse and a tinge of fear. Will Pax come after me now or does white guilt still protect me from his views of justice?

"Is that true?" Fetty asks the silent Pax.

Pax moves his gaze from Fetty and the sunlight back to the coals of the fire. He stares at it for a long time, reliving whatever hell he went through.

"I did kill Kevin…" he says to the fire. "I smashed his head in with the butt of my rifle while the soldiers chased us into the burning forest. I did it for many reasons—jealousy, justice, fear—but mainly…I killed Kevin because he wanted me to."

PAX STANDS up and takes a step toward his oven. He picks up a fire-hardened stick and moves the coals around, then flips them over, exposing the hot underbelly to more oxygen. They shimmer and shine then ignite little flames that lick the remaining goat meat.

"After we left the campfire and our first slaughter of the lamb, we stomped off into the night, and Kevin kept teasing me. He said he knew about…about the fact that I was seeing things that weren't there…that I thought my sister Vivi was in Tajikistan with us, and he goaded me on, that maybe I just imagined I killed those other teenagers."

He stops staring at the fire and looks to Lupina, to all of us with his admission of weakness. *He was seeing things that weren't there.* Can we trust anything he says?

"I thought he knew because Lupina told him. She was the only person I admitted this to, and she, you…you were trying to help me…you understood me and didn't judge me."

"Pax, I never said a word to anyone, I promise you."

"I know. I know…the next day, on the way to see the bodies of the teenagers I killed near the road, he started talking about the battle and everything after, about how, yes, he did swap the sheep for destroying the base. In many ways, that's not so bad; the National Guard was evil, anyway. But he admitted to calling the other base in Afghanistan on the radio, taunting them, daring them to come attack us. I know he did it to pit the other base against the local tribe, but it seemed like a huge risk that resulted in Sam getting killed. It could have killed us all, really, and when I confronted him on it, he just smiled his stupid emo smile and said 'all you can do is play counting coup with death.'

"That ate me up inside. We all knew that Kevin had suicidal tendencies, but to take risks with all of us, with Lupina, my sister…just joking, but all of us, The Tribe of Iodine Wine, was very dangerous."

"So, you killed him?" Charlotte asks.

"No, not yet. It was the next day, after we crossed into the burning forest, near our second battle, where Sam died and I killed the kids. We were attacked. Soldiers from the other base sprung on us, but we fought them off and escaped through the smoke and flames. I decided to skip showing him the bodies of the teenagers I killed. I had nothing to prove to that psycho, I just wanted to get back to the tribe, to Lupina. I thought Kevin agreed, but when we were sneaking back through the forest fire we spotted some of the other soldiers. They didn't see us, so I thought we were safe, but Kevin attacked them anyway. All crazy, he just charged at them."

Pax takes a deep breath before he continues.

"I...helped. I flanked them and we took a few down but when reinforcements came we had to flee again. During our escape, Kevin kept provoking them, kept betraying our location, yelling out, firing shots...so that is when I killed him. Bashed his head in, because I was scared, because I thought I was never going to see you again. Because he kept playing counting coup with death and included me—us—in his stupid game."

Tears are in Pax's eyes, heavy and dark, with the murder of his best friend. Lupina embraces him but he continues to just stare out past Fetty, past the entrance to the cave and the bright white light in the distance.

"Suicide by Pax," he says. "I realized, after everything, he wanted me to kill him. That's why he was egging me on: he saw his death as my birth into manhood."

"Pax, you can't know that; he was just a crazy kid, doing crazy shit," Jaden says.

Lupina lets go of Pax and turns to her friends. "Oh no, we know that. Kevin wrote Pax a suicide note, penned it on the map he left Pax showing the path back to me, to the village we renamed Caxm. But you never followed the map," she says, turning to Pax, sad and forlorn.

"No, I never followed the map, only the example."

7

CHEKOV'S GUN

❧

The gravity of the words, the gravity of the final truth about Kevin pushes down on us like a cave-in. Pax just keeps staring at the fire while Lupina rubs his back with one hand and offers him her water with another.

He breaks out of his trance and looks at the dirty water. "Are you still drinking iodate water?" he asks.

"Nope, we are saving the iodine for wounds now."

"Good. It's toxic, you know; the way you were doing it before; the way we did it for the Ceremony of our tribe," he says with a shake of his head.

"To the Tribe of Iodine Wine," he says, then takes a long swig.

"Kevin told me mixing that much medicinal iodine with water can cause issues with our thyroids. Not sure if anyone had any side-effects, during the escape or fighting; adrenaline is a powerful panacea, I guess. But Kevin thought it was funny, our Ceremony and the sharing of iodine wine. I thought it was creepy that he knew that—not about the properties of iodine, but about the

Ceremony, the oath we all took for protection because he wasn't there for it. And do you know how he knew?"

"He was spying on us," Fetty says.

"Yep. That's how I know he was lying about Lupina betraying my secret. He was spying on us. But how did you know that, Fetty?"

"When I snuck back into the base, I set up a blind in our old barracks, in the attic, so I could scope out the soldiers. While I was there I saw the cell phones he was using to record our conversations. Some were still working, and I knew they were Kevin's and knew he was spying on us too."

"You went back to the base?" Pax asks.

"Yeah, I destroyed it. Burnt it to the ground."

"And the kids, the ones left behind?"

Now it's Fetty's turn to stare at the fire. She takes a breath. I get the impression that Charlotte, Jaden, and Lupina already know the story. They probably talked about it when I was at the turret on top of the truck. What other stories and plans did they discuss?

"They were starving. They were also being…being eaten by the soldiers. After I burned down the barracks and shot the remaining guardsmen, I killed a buck for them, stumbled on Kevin's body when I was hunting it, but when I offered the venison to the kids, they looked at me with scorn and…and ate the soldiers that cooked in the fire."

She stops talking again and just dead-eye stares into Pax's oven. And I now I understand why Fetty has changed so much; from the flight to the forest, to the hunting of men, to destroying the base and seeing the teenagers eat dead bodies, Fetty has witnessed more depravity than any us. She has bathed in the bloody waters of the Red Wave.

"So, you just left them?" Lily asks.

"Yes."

Those were Lily's classmates and friends. Maybe Fetty should have stayed and helped. Maybe she should have rounded us up so we could help escort them to Caxm. Maybe this is a fool's errand, but if Fetty had helped the teenagers, we wouldn't have made it to Badakhshan and found Lily and Pax.

"We have one goal right now," Lupina offers. "We wanted to find Pax and save those girls. Let's get across the river and finish the objective. Then we can go back to the forest."

"Hmmm. Maybe they don't want to be saved," Lily says.

"We need to give them that option. We need to know, too, for ourselves."

"Well, then, let's get across that river," Pax says.

WE WALK down river with supplies and a new-found hope as we near the end of this impossible mission and the crossing into Afghanistan. At a promontory of rocks overlooking the river, Pax stops.

"See, hidden under the trees. Boats." Pax points downriver a bit to a small hut and outcropping of river trees.

"They're on the other side," Jaden says.

"I'll get them," I volunteer. They think I am being chivalrous and daring, but if I fetch the boats then I can carry my gun across.

"Can you even swim?"

I give Jaden the side-eye. He knows I can swim, knows that I love jokes about black stereotypes, too, I guess. But then I wonder if Jaden can swim.

I start to strip myself of my ordinance, my shirt, shoes, and swatches of the felt robe. My shoulders feel polished, hard, ready for this. My legs too, are like columns of stone after our trek through Badakhshan carrying my heavy weight. I head down to the river.

"Hey, Michael, we are going to head downriver a bit," Pax says. "It will take you quite some distance to get back across."

"I'll stay here and watch over Michael," Lupina says.

"Me too." Lily offers, and the other women stay on the rocks while Jaden and Pax head downriver.

I reach the water and start to have doubts about my path. Even though it is late in the season, the water is still tumultuous and cold, and the other bank looks like a far-off foreign shore, which it technically is. I also realize, I probably won't make it across. There is no encouragement or second thoughts from the ladies behind me, and I can't help but think that some of them may have stayed behind to watch me die.

I turn around. Over the rumbling water I yell, "I'm sorry, Lily, for what I did. I was caught up in the battle, caught up in my revenge...for what they did to me, but I was wrong. I shouldn't have done that...I should have stopped Kevin."

She looks at me with Charlotte, Fetty, and Lupina by her side. She considers her words carefully, then glances at Fetty.

"No worries. Sounds like I avoided a worse path. You know, at least I didn't have to resort to cannibalism...or be the victim of it."

I start walking more into the Panj. The cold takes my breath away as the water works up my body. I stop for a few more seconds and breathe, to acclimate to the frigid temperature, then lumber forward with my strong legs.

I am about a third of the way across when the water becomes too high for me to walk. The current is so strong that it will soon sweep me off my feet. I stop and prepare myself for the swim. I glance back over my shoulder at the women on the bank, huddled, it seems, in prayer and anticipation. I just hope they are praying for my safety.

I look to the other bank and pick a line, then dive forward. The river instantly takes me downstream, and I know, even if I make it across, I will overshoot the boats.

I decide to not worry about path and trajectories and put my face into the cold water and just motor forward. My shoulders feel good, my legs feel strong, and I make good progress churning my legs and plunging my arms over and over in the water.

But with a third of the way left, I am already far away from the women and can hear Jaden and Pax yelling encouragement from way upstream. My *strong* legs are burning; my shoulders ache. Swimming in the current is a totally different exercise new to my muscles. I start to tire and can feel myself slipping under the water, having more and more trouble getting my mouth to the surface for a breath. The rapids are more intense now, and I feel all is lost.

I decide to relax, to let river take me. I move my feet under my butt and just start to float with the rapids. With my head above the water, I catch my breath and point my feet downstream as buffers against the rocks and use the break to recover, use my hands to try to navigate me to the other side.

I see a bend in the river and head for the eddy, aiming for the banks. When I am about ready to pass out, I have a novel thought. It seeps into my mind in an old lady voice, maybe my grandmother, maybe Anahita.

"Stand up, boy," I hear. "Stand up."

I put my feet down and touch river sand. Then I rise up tall and walk my way to the shore.

HOURS LATER, we are all safe and huddled on the Afghani side of the Panj. I feel fatigued, but recovering, whole again, now that I am fairly dry with my gun and rocket boxes of ammo in their familiar position centered around my body.

Night is starting to fall and the cold is making others, still chilled from the rough row across the river, shake and shudder. They huddle close to each other, but despite my heroics I still feel like an outsider. I sit off to the side, not needing their collective warmth; my muscles, hard-pressed on the swim across and paddling back and forth, are hot with use.

"Now what?" Lupina asks.

Everyone seems too cold or tired to answer, but she's right; we were focusing so much on the impossible journey that we didn't consider what to do once we reached the goal.

"I kept seeing tribe members with villagers come down to the river, so they're probably a few clicks in," Pax says.

"How far is a click?" Jaden asks.

"Well, pardner," Pax says in a western cowboy accent, "I don't really know, I just like the way it sounds."

The joke is needed, warms us up like a campfire.

"Ok, so they're close?"

"Yeah, an hour or two away."

"So, now what?" Lupina repeats. "Are we just going in there guns blazing like a bunch of cowboys? Is that really the plan?"

Even though I have the biggest, most powerful gun, she looks to Pax and Fetty for confirmation, but they both just shake their heads.

"We won't be able to get close to them," Pax says.

"What?" Jaden asks.

"It's true," Fetty agrees.

"Oh, yeah, people of the forest…."

"Or desert or whatever, they are of the wilderness, and they expect an attack, at all times," Fetty says. "Look, we could attack the men from the National Guard, and win, because they never expected it of us. They just viewed us as younger, lesser versions of the themselves. But we are special, elite, and the government picked us for a reason, and we proved it. But we cannot sneak up on that tribe. We cannot surprise them, and if we attack, we will probably lose."

"Awesome, so what the fuck is the plan?"

"I was just hoping we could track them from a distance for a few days," Pax says. "And try to spot one of the girls, give a signal, maybe, and they'll escape like Lily did. Then we can pick them up."

"I didn't escape," Lily says.

"You didn't?" Lupina asks.

"No, I didn't want to marry the man they had for me. He already had a wife, and just wasn't my type, ha. So, they let me leave."

"They let you leave? I thought you were sold."

"Oh my god, I am not for sale! I explained this to your friends while you were getting busy in the cave."

"What about the other girls? Were they sold?"

"OK, listen and listen carefully: we slept with the guys from the National Guard because we wanted to, not because we were selling ourselves for favors, not because we were forced. They were older, strong, good looking. They had real confidence—not wannabe-rapper swagger—but you all made assumptions about me, about us, that somehow spun us into whores, into literal prostitutes, both on the base and with the tribe.

"But what *really* sucks," she says and looks straight at me. "Is you thought it *was* true, that we were being sold for sex, and you did it anyway."

"So, the other girls are happy with the Afghani tribe?" Lupina asks, to slide the conversation back on track.

"I'm not totally sure. I left early on, then Pax picked me up. He said he would take me back to the base after his big rescue mission. He had food and a map, so I stuck with him, thinking I might be able to help, too. Kelly was sick when I left, but I think Becky was warming up to her suitor."

"OK, awesome, so you weren't sold, and Becky and Kelly aren't owned."

"Yep, the tribe was actually pretty nice, just not my cup of tea."

With this, Lupina stands up and starts throwing her hands around and pointing at all of us. "People, we really need to fucking communicate. Pax, you run off knowing what you know about Kevin and the girls and the base and don't tell anyone. Fetty, you suspect Pax of betraying us and don't say anything. Lily, you left the tribe with their permission and never mentioned it to Pax or us, and we all, like Lily said, just assumed this was part of some sex slavery sale. Because now, we were about to walk into a firefight with the people of the forest/desert/wilderness, whatever, a battle we'll lose, and we *don't* have to fight them."

"What do you mean?"

"If the girls aren't owned, we don't have to steal them. We can just talk to them and the tribe!" She points this out like a teacher lecturing her students.

"We don't speak their language."

"Becky and Kelly probably know enough by now. Fuck, guys, less fighting more talking."

AFTER A COLD, huddled night eager with hope, we wake and head inland and within an hour walk right into their sentries. They seem to materialize out of the rock, with dress and turbans the color of sand and dirt carrying AK-47s as worn as the land. We found ourselves surrounded, and despite Lupina's speech, our guns are up and ready for battle. They yell at us from behind rocks and guns as more and more of their friends show up.

Fetty has stayed behind, disappeared in the night as an insurance policy, and I wonder if they have found her too. And if not, can she help us with the element of surprise once the bullets start flying.

As soon as they appeared, Jaden, Charlotte, and I split up. They seem to only focus their guns on us, on me, especially, so I back my way into a V in a boulder and get ready to fire. My muzzle moves back and forth and anyone who gets in the path shirks back.

So concerned with my gun and the guns being raised against me that I don't pay attention to our unarmed friends. While moving my sight back and forth, I see Lupina and Lily, holding hands, standing on a rock. They are waving and smiling at the tribe, totally exposed and unprotected. I watch from my crevice until finally one of the tribesmen walks up, takes a close look at Lily and laughs. He yells something back at his friends and a cackle of laughter breaks out all around the rocks, echoing off the stones and valley as a portly man with a big moustache waddles up to the boulders to say hi. If he was wearing green or red overalls, I would expect him to bounce up the rocks to video game dings.

But I stay in my crevice even after Jaden and Charlotte have eased their weapons down and joined Lupina and Lily and her old suitor on the rock. I can't help but feel it's comical, the look on his face, like a teenage boy wondering if his crush has changed her mind.

"Michael, it's OK," Lupina says.

I stand up and step out from my rock and look over my shoulder at two tribesmen, positioned on the rock right behind, waiting for me to fire.

A few minutes later Becky shows up, wearing local garb and a hard, tan face. She smiles and hugs Lily and even embraces Lupina. She looks us all over, but her smile slips away when she sees me.

"Welcome back," she says to Lily. "They think you changed your mind. Have you?"

"Ha, that's what I figured. No, we just wanted to see if you or Kelly changed yours."

"You all came down here for that?"

"Yeah, they felt guilty about what happened."

"Ah, the good old bleeding heart," she says with a chuckle.

At this, one of the tribal leaders comes into the conversation. I recognize the big, scruffy man from when Kevin, Eva, and I traded lies for sheep. He isn't smiling. He looks us all over, paying special attention to Jaden and I. Then he focuses on me. He remembers me from the trade when I fired a warning shot over his head.

He says something in Wakhi to Becky.

She turns to me. "You can't come into his lands armed. You are guests, not invaders."

I just give a shrug and say, "We're ready to leave. Let him know why we are here."

They have a long debate. Becky's words seem broken, pidgin, and she uses her hands a lot.

Finally, with anger, he turns and yells commands to his soldiers. A couple of them come over and bring bowls and thermoses. He motions to us to sit down, and everyone gathers in a circle around Becky and her leader, but I stay near my rock with guns still on me. They drink tea while we wait.

As soon as the tea is passed, Fetty, to her credit, pops up over a boulder and slips into the circle for a bowl. The sentries look ashamed at Fetty's stealth and get chewed out by their leader. I stay back, and even though I can smell the tea and it reminds me of my time with Anahita, I avoid the cordialities.

Half-way through their tea time, Kelly comes up to our circle. She is leaning on a local woman, limping on one foot, and her face looks sickly.

"He says you can take Kelly back, but for a price."

"I thought you weren't sold," Lupina says to Lily and Becky.

"We weren't," Becky responds. "But Kelly is weak and unmarried and has been living off the tribe. That needs to be paid for."

"We don't have any money."

"A trade then."

We look at each other, checking out our weak supplies and gear. Finally, Lupina, then everyone, focuses on me. Why are they looking at me? Is this my final penance? The rough baptism in the Panj wasn't enough? An eye for an eye!

Fuck that shit. I yelled out a promise by the flagpole: "Never Again." And I don't care what I have done, I will not be subjugated, enslaved, or traded even if they think it is deserved.

Let me ride the Red Wave, embrace it as a truly holy baptism. I feel an urge to cover myself in blood. To cock my gun and let loose on Lupina and my other so-called *friends* who think justice is selling me into slavery. I will slaughter them all and the girls I carry guilt about; then the well-armed militia and I can fight it out and decide between their leader, Fetty, and I, who should run Badassastan.

I feel the blood-rage boil within me as I slip into a trance, like the night of the Battle of Base when we started the killing game, and I plunged my knife through the corporal's chest. I feel euphoric. I cock my gun.

"Michael, Michael!" I hear Jaden yell and jump toward me. He places himself in front of my muzzle. "She means your gun. Your *gun*! Not you, for fuck's sake, man."

I stare at him and blink my eyes a couple of times. I can feel the kill-trance start to slip away. The Red Wave ebbs back.

"Michael, did you think I wanted to trade you for Becky?" Lupina asks.

I can only nod.

"Wow, I'm sorry you feel that way," she says. "But I would never...never harm you."

She comes up to me and places her hands on my arms, still tense from the near battle, she rubs them to stop the shaking.

"Michael, how could you think that?"

"There are only two kinds of white people: those who patronize us and those who are counting backward to zero. I started to think you were the latter."

"I am neither," she says, tersely. "But it's time to give up that gun."

PEACE PRIZE

L ike some sad ceremony, I reluctantly strip myself of the gun and ammo I carried hundreds of miles. I feel both liberated and exposed at the same time.

Charlotte comes over and starts fastening Fetty's cord and Anahita's felt fabric to me, into a large harness to wear on my back.

"Kelly is sick and has a broken ankle. You have to carry her back to the Humvee. That's your penance, but hey, at least carrying all that weaponry got you in good shape."

I stand there helpless, lifeless as Charlotte lectures me and quickly constructs her new costume, but with every measure and tie I feel a burden lift from me. She is right; this is the path to redemption.

"So, Michael can carry Kelly," Lupina says to Becky. "But are you ready to make the journey? Did you need to gather anything from the village?"

"And where are you going? Do you have a one-way ticket back to the States stashed in your medicine bag?"

My new-found forgiveness prompts me to jump into the

conversation, to lead and brag. "We have a village, a peaceful village. We coexist with locals under an orchard and in yurts, where we share sheep, fruit, safety."

Becky gives an eye-raise showing some interest.

"Um...we don't have a village," Lupina says.

"Say what?" I ask.

"Before I destroyed the base," Fetty says. "I watched from my blind as Eva came with someone else from our tribe and made a deal with some soldiers. They all left together in three Humvees. I can only assume they went to Caxm and took over. After what I did to Eva, throwing her from her horse, and with Pax killing Kevin, there is no safety in Caxm for us."

"She betrayed us to exert control," Lupina says.

Wait. What the actual fuck? Caxm is lost. Anahita and her villagers, who took us in, who fed and cared for us, are now under the soldiers' authority. Why am I learning about this now? We should have attacked them first, then gone on this stupid mission. And wait, how did Lupina know?

Then it hits me — when I was exiled to the turret they talked about the base and Caxm and left me out of the loop.

"You knew? You knew Caxm was compromised and didn't say anything. I thought we were supposed to communicate!" I yell at Lupina. "You were my only friend since leaving Anahita, and now she is under the rule of cannibals and slavers."

"Back off, Michael," Pax says. And Fetty, too, gets between Lupina and me.

I feel the blood-rage come back. Everything goes red, and then I lunge. I go straight for Fetty and punch her in the chest. My fist cracks through the stupid deer skull fastened to her stupid deer cape on top of her stupid vinyl outfit.

The skull splits, and she stumbles back and both she and Lupina are knocked down, but I keep coming. I rip Fetty's rifle out of her hands and toss it to the rocks, then lift her up off the ground to well-above my head.

"You're not the Queen of Badassastan!" I yell up at her. "You don't get to decide who lives and dies."

Then I slam her back to the ground and press my knee into her, to subjugate her, to show her the full force of a man, to show her who is really in charge.

"That's enough, Michael! You get off her right now or I will end you," a strong female voice commands.

I look up and see Charlotte's slingshot loaded and pulled back, aiming right at my temple.

I just keep breathing hard and return my stare into Fetty's eyes. She, somehow, looks calm, collected.

"Now!" Charlotte orders.

I slowly let go of Fetty and stand up. I turn around and fetch her gun. Now that I am armed again, Pax, Jaden, and Charlotte have their weapons trained on me. But I just sling the rifle over my shoulder.

The warriors from the militia are watching the spectacle through laughs and grins, but I don't care. I only have one goal now, to get back to Caxm and save our tribe, save Anahita and her tribe. This truly was a fool's errand, a failure of a mission, even if we found Pax.

"We're leaving; we're freeing Caxm," I command.

"Yeah, nah, I'm going to stay here with Becky and the tribe," Kelly says. "But good luck with all that."

Her snarky words give me hope that I can get my munitions back, but they are taken, folded into the militia for no value in trade.

"Fine. You were too much weight anyway," I say and stomp off.

The adrenaline starts to wane as I march away from the circle and back onto the boulders. I turn and see who is still with me. Lupina and Pax are hiking up the rocks behind me. Her bangs now covers her eyes, and they look to the ground. Jaden and Charlotte are back with Fetty, helping her up. Jaden takes his rifle and offers it to Fetty, knowing she is deadlier with it. His gesture makes my behavior and words seem chauvinistic and churlish, but so what.

Fetty stands up and stretches her back with arms wide and spreads her shoulders like one of her crows spreading its wings. She looks down at the deer skull, fractured across her chest then shrugs with her knife clutched in her hand. She wipes the knife tip off on the broken skull and tucks it away then gives Jaden her pistol and takes his rifle with a nod.

I keep watching them and Lily to see which way they will choose, but they all just turn my way, with heads down like beaten and guilty dogs, and follow us up the rocks. Lily, too, gives Becky and Kelly hugs and words then joins the rest of our group.

I turn back around and lead our journey back to Caxm, back toward the Panj and Tajikistan. As I walk I press my hand to the soft side-belly beneath my ribs, to the trickle of blood from Fetty's knife point.

WE REACH THE BOATS, and I decide the price of my armaments is passage across the river without having to swim. I will not be returning their boat to the Afghani side.

"Get in. We'll paddle the boat across and leave it on the other side," I tell the group, and they follow.

"Yay, we bought a boat," Jaden says.

We ignore him.

I am so over their self-righteous condemnation of me when they lost Caxm, our home. Or the moral decision to strand the teenagers on the base to starvation and suffering. After the battle, still wrapped up in the revenge and blood-rage, yes, I followed Kevin into the forest and made a mistake, but what have they done? We are homeless, friendless, and missed our true path to redemption, upholding the oath we made at the Ceremony.

I'm dragging the hidden boat back down to the water when I feel a tug. I turn around and see Lupina holding the other end of the boat, trying to be steady against my pull. There are tears in her eyes and everyone is watching us, wondering if this a battle for leadership, a battle for our path.

"I'm sorry, Michael, that I didn't tell you about Eva and Caxm. Fetty did tell us, but I thought with all your time in the Humvee, with your self-exile and morbidity...I wasn't sure that you cared, but that was no excuse. I was wrong, and you were right. I should have communicated, but you shouldn't have attacked Fetty. Our greatest strength is our solidarity."

She lets go of the boat and turns to face everyone else.

"And I was wrong to lead us on this mission. I was too caught up, too obsessed with finding Pax...on finding the love of my life, that I didn't think of our oath and the greater good. Michael was right. We should have fought for our tribes and Caxm, and we need to fight for them now."

9

STEPPENWOLVES

~

L ight without the burden of the munitions but heavy with the burden of obligation, I pushed our group hard and days later, we reached the Humvee. Many hours after, we ran out of gas, but with Fetty's suggestion we completed our hike to her nest for resupply and rest.

Lupina traces her fingers along a faded rope strung across the outcropping of boulders. She stops at each tied cord marking the line and flicks the frayed end of different colored tassels.

"This is the story of us?" Lupina asks.

Fetty is busy getting gear together. She uncovers tarps like ripping Christmas wrapping paper, revealing the weapons and supplies she took from the soldiers she killed: rifles, grenades, MREs that she never touched, but no .50 calibers. She stops her unwrapping and looks to Lupina.

"The story of some of us, a timeline, to help answer some questions."

"Ah, Pax's betrayal and Michael's crime. Both false, in certain ways."

"Both true, in certain ways."

To add a challenge to the debate, Fetty picks up a rifle, checks it for wear and rounds, then walks over to Lupina and holds out the gun. Lupina ducks and spins under the rope, putting it between them.

"No, thanks. I'm a lover not a fighter," she says and pats her medical bag.

"You might not have the luxury of that choice if we lose."

"We will always have that choice."

Lily, claiming a hunting past with her dad, has climbed one of the boulders and is scouting the surroundings with a sniper rifle Fetty provided. Jaden, rearmed now, inspects the boulders, their size, the distance between. You can tell he is architecting a grand castle, a new home, maybe. Charlotte does not opt for a gun but keeps her slingshot close, stocked with metal projectiles. She is stitching together more proper clothes taken from Fetty's cache, some still adorned with blood and bullet holes, but the right color for camouflage in the forests north of Badakhshan.

Lily looks up from her scope and turns to Fetty and Lupina, still facing off.

"You know, my dad taught me a lot of things. How to hunt, how to change a tire, how to terrorize your wife and family."

We all stop and look up at her.

"I thought a lot about that in the wilderness. If there's one thing the desert does, it purifies your thoughts. Runs them through a sandy filter. Like, just because a crime wasn't committed, doesn't mean Eva, Michael, and Kevin weren't immoral. Just because we didn't need saving, doesn't mean Pax isn't a hero. But I thought a lot about my path and how I ended up where I ended.

"My older sister was a lesbian…is a lesbian, fuck, I don't even know if she is still alive….Well, either way, she *is* a lesbian. I used to think her sexuality was an act of rebellion, defiance against an abusive and overbearing dad to forswear all men. I took an opposite pathos, ha; my response was to seek objectifying attention and older men. But, I was naïve at the time, didn't realize my sister was never boy crazy, was always a tomboy, always attracted to females. I just thought she found safety in love from women because they wouldn't beat her. Then one beat her, nearly within an inch of her life. Found out after that lesbian relationships have higher abuse rates than heterosexual ones. And homosexual males have the lowest abuse rates. Thought about that a lot in Badakhshan. It's not so much about the violence of men as it is the violent way we view women."

Her eyes focus on us, then fix on me as if she is looking at me through a scope.

"See, the reason you all thought we were being sold, the reason why you, Michael, thought it was fine for us to be sold, is because we don't value women. We treat them as property—my dad did, my sister's girlfriend did, and you, Kevin, and Eva did. So even if your crime wasn't a crime, you're still guilty. But you've paid your dues, repented your ways. I forgive you. But I don't forgive Eva."

She goes back to her scope and scans the plains again.

"Look," she says from up on her boulder perch, and we all go on alert, weapons up. "Are those dogs?"

Down the hill from our rocks, a pack of canines are sniffing around in the dead grass. They throw glances to our rocks in a curious, unafraid manner.

"No, wolves from the steppe," Fetty says. "I used to keep them and their crow friends well fed."

"They're probably glad you're back," Lupina says. Fetty looks at her with a face so blank I can't tell if she wants to kill her or laugh, or both.

"Here, speaking of reuniting old friends, why don't you take your rifle back," I say and offer her the gun I took from her days before in Afghanistan, an offer, a peace prize.

Fetty turns her blank stare toward me.

"I shouldn't have attacked you. I'm sorry I took it," I say.

She swaps the unwanted rifle she was going to give Lupina for her familiar gun, running her fingers over it like a musician with their favorite instrument. "I am sorry you lost your big gun. We actually need it now," she says.

"What are they digging at?" Lupina asks.

Fetty and I turn back to the plains, at the wolves scrounging around in the dirt.

"Oh, when I was resting here one day, a group of soldiers tried to sneak up on me. I did not see them or hear them. They were crawling through the grass. They knew I was here and were coming to kill me. My crows alerted me to the attack," she says, and we are all transfixed. "We had a...an agreement, the crows and I. They alerted me to prey and received the kill-bounty in return. Anyway, I snuck out the back, came around behind them while they crawled and shot them all. Then the birds flew off to get the wolves. See, crows cannot tear apart a carcass; they can only pick at it. Pick, pick, pick." She moves her fingers from the worn touch-stone stock of her gun to mimic a crow picking at flesh. "The wolves came and ripped away at the remains, so the crows could get more food. I guess, they also have an agreement. Anyway, I think the wolves are digging at the bones left by the kill and feast."

"Man, you don't talk much, but when you do, you've got some crazy stories to tell," Lily says from the rocks above.

"Yes, charming, but we need to bury what remains," Lupina says.

"We've dug enough fucking holes," Jaden says.

"We bury them, Jaden. Bring your shovel."

Lupina starts to walk toward the wolves unarmed, unafraid. Pax jumps up to guard her, but she moves forward until she is in between the bones and the pack, resting on their haunches, watching Lupina with an amused curiosity.

LATER, under the stars, brightened by a campfire, we have our own feast. We chance the fire since it may be our last supper, the day before our attack on Caxm. To save water, we just brush the dirt and bone dust off our hands and crack open the MREs.

We relish in processed food so different from our flavorless, sun-dried small game. We all start with dessert first.

"Mmm, I've missed chocolate," Charlotte says with a rare smile.

Fetty, too, forces a smile like a struggling parent who gives her children more Christmas presents than she can afford.

There are no more words spoken until we have finished the meals and thrown the trash into the fire. We all sit back, satiated, and watch the plastic and paper burn in unnatural colors.

"So, I've been thinking of a plan, a strategy," Lupina says. An awkward silence hangs in the air, but no one says what we are all thinking, that a peaceful approach will not work for Caxm. We can't gain reentry into the village with a dictionary and herd of sheep this time. Eva will never give up control and even if she considers a truce, according to Fetty, there are at least ten to twenty depraved and murderous soldiers whose friends we slaughtered. I start to formulate a rebuke to the negatives of seeking peace.

"Well, we need a serious assessment of all our strengths," Lupina says. "Pax and Fetty can run fast and are…good with their weapons. They should…what's it called, when you sneak behind the enemy? Like what Fetty did with the crawling soldiers."

"Flank."

"Yes, they should flank Caxm, sneak around back while Jaden, Charlotte, and Michael start a frontal attack."

"What about me? These people butchered and ate my friends," Lily says.

"Well, I was thinking about you. See, they don't know about you. They also don't know that we met back up with Pax and Fetty, so even if the frontal attack fails…and we get caught or killed, you three, especially you, Lily, can still launch surprise attacks."

"Damn, that's some cold ass shit, coming from the warmest heart among us," Jaden says.

"Well, the thing about being sensitive," Fetty says. "When you understand another's strengths and weaknesses, you know best how to hurt them."

"Thanks, I guess. Anyway, speaking of strengths, with Charlotte's penchant for stealth, and her slingshot, we are going to try to make our way far into Caxm without detection. Dispensing as many people as we can, silently. Pax, Fetty, and Lily, as soon as gunfire breaks out, you start, but not before, unless you can be quiet about it. Michael, you can try to make your way to the big guns, but keep in mind they will probably expect that. Understand?" she says with confidence.

Everyone nods in shock. And I chuckle at the similarities between her plan and Kevin's at the Battle of the Base. But Pax just looks at the fire, lost deep in its blaze.

"One question: who are we killing?" he asks.

"Um, the enemy."

"Who are we killing?" he repeats. "The enemy? Who are they? Are we shooting Eva? Are we cool with killing our friend? Fetty, you down with that?"

She nods, and he continues. "What if our other friends are armed? I mean the soldiers, that's easy, right? They're cannibals and slavers, as Michael said. But what if Cisco has a gun? Is Spencer still armed? Lupina, you mentioned he may have a baby now, Felicia, too. I bet they're keen on protecting their babies. Are we killing all of them? Babies, too?"

"No, no babies," Lupina says, shocked and deflated, and trying to recover. "You made a good point, Pax. We'll send scouts first. Thanks for volunteering. Fetty, will you join him?"

After the fire dies down, we go to an uneasy sleep in nests around the boulders. Jaden has stopped his architecting of the monoliths and just stares straight up at the stars framed by the big rocks, like all of us, with thoughts of babies and wolves and cannibals and the world we now live in.

10

THE BATTLE OF CAXM

~

The next night, eager and scared, we camp underneath the distant view of the mountain crest they crossed into Caxm months earlier, near the shipwreck rock, where I found my friends on the way back out.

Our sleep is uneasy and incomplete. Pax and Fetty snuck out into the dark to scope the approaches into Caxm. After tossing and turning, I sit up and take a comfortable lean against a tree. In the distance, I can see the crest and the huge protruding rock. I look at the boulder then back to my friends, Jaden, Charlotte, Lupina, and Lily cuddled together under the lean-to. The nights are much colder, up north, and high up in the forested mountains. My breath shrouds my vision of the shelter and far off crest in a mist of ghostly white.

I am staring out with a heavy heart. Tomorrow's battle looms over us like specter. We are going to attack our friends. We have no idea who is on Eva's side and who is under her thumb. This isn't an unknown Afghani tribe that we can cast as *the other*, as terrorists. This isn't traitorous American soldiers who tried to rape Fetty and whipped and…and…and, I can say it now: who raped me.

This is our tribe, people we made the journey with, made an oath with, fought and died with. My only hope is that Fetty and Pax's scouting can offer some kind of differentiation between friend and foe, a color-coded video game guide showing who to shoot and who not to shoot.

But that is not the case. Pax, quiet and quick, slips back into our camp soon after leaving. "We need to go," he tells me as if offering a snippet of a secret he is eager to spread. "Wake everyone up."

"What happened?"

"The killing started. Sentries were at the crest, the pass where you went through before. Fetty impulsively and silently killed them, but they were part of a watch. They may be due back in Caxm or have replacements soon. We need to start the attack before we are found out."

"Were they…were they soldiers or friends?" I ask.

"Soldiers."

I get up and follow Pax to the lean-to. He goes to the side Lily and Lupina are cuddled on while I wake Jaden and Charlotte.

WE MEET Fetty at the crest, under the shipwreck rock, where two soldiers sit with stab wounds in their hearts and slit throats cascading drying blood out over their punctured chests like waterfalls into a pool. They are cast aside, hunted animals, and I can't help but wonder if the steppenwolves and crows will find them.

Fetty dons the weird camouflage costume again, over layers of foam, vinyl, and blood. The branches and leaves poke out like ruffled feathers as she squats, in a corvid-like stance, above us on one of the big rocks, ready to spring at any replacements coming up from Caxm.

"No scouting. We will just have to go straight in," she tells us while looking ahead. Her face seems to be in a trance; she is back in the Red Wave. "But I have watched them from a distance. They seem to be dulled, probably thinking we are gone for good. If we hit quick and precise we can take out most of them before they can react."

She jumps down from the boulder, and we are off. Pax sprints forward to keep up with Fetty, but turns around to give Lupina a longing, childish look, reminding me of how he looked when we first came to Tajikistan.

And then they are gone. Charlotte, Jaden, Lily and I run forward with Lupina trailing us, unarmed still. I want to stop and give her something to defend herself, but it may be more dangerous to have someone wielding an unsure weapon behind us.

Jaden and I break away from the women as we sprint downhill. "You check the yurts, I'm going to try to get a .50 caliber," I say. Jaden's uneasiness with violence should lower the chances of him shooting one of our friends, and if I take a big gun I should, at least, be the last man standing.

Before we are even close to the village, we hear muffled explosions ring out as Fetty drops grenades in their defenses, and now, Caxm is alive with yelling and gunfire, quick, exact shots that seem to cascade up the village. The return fire seems weak and dies quickly in its place which gives me hope. Still, I head for the Humvees and my old dark, tree branch cavern.

I pass a couple of dead soldiers on the way there but see no other enemies. I move forward, more cautious, stepping toward my familiar haunt. Behind me I hear a familiar voice yelling.

"It's Jaden. Stay in your yurts! Stay in your yurts!" he yells, both scared and commanding at the same time.

There are more shots fired near the fields, a frantic exchange of gunfire and an explosion. Then Charlotte calls out between the clangs and rattle of her slingshot.

"Lupina, Lupina! Fetty is down."

My heart starts to race. I move forward faster, lunging toward the cave and the guns. Our best protector is down. I feel vulnerable, scared; I reach t h e darkened arbor and scurry up the Humvee, but the gun is gone. I look to the other Humvees, but they are just weaponless, emasculated vehicles. They must have set up the .50 caliber in the foxholes Fetty took out with the grenades.

"Don't fucking move, Michael," I hear Eva say.
She comes out of the shadows, shouldered by two soldiers.
"You piece of shit, I can't believe you came back. Caxm is mine now."

There are three guns trained on me, and I don't have time or a chance to move my rifle. I just slide it down to the empty turret and put my hands up. I am caught, captured, even before I had a chance to contribute, to take an enemy down. Eva walks toward me like a queen.

"Who is with you? How many are attacking?" she asks and raises her muzzle to point it directly at my face. "You have five seconds to answer."

Two shots ring out close and for a split second I think I am dead, that the five second timer was just an evil joke by Eva, but then I see the soldiers fall, and Pax sprints up behind Eva.

"Put it down, Eva. Don't make me kill you."
Eva just keeps staring at me. She looks like she is weighing her choice, killing us both or giving up. I know she is too selfish to go down in a blaze of glory; she just shuts her eyes and lowers the muzzle. We have won. The battle is over, and we have captured Eva.

"Pax! Pax, what the hell are you doing?" From behind, a familiar, commanding voice yells out. "Lower your weapon, now!"

I look up, outside of the shadows, past Eva and Pax, to something that is impossible. Pax slowly turns to look, too, then collapses, crestfallen, to the ground.

"No, no, it can't be," he whines like a child. And for the second time that night, someone calls out for Lupina. "I thought I was good. Lupina! Lupina! I thought I was good."

In the distance, rougher, bearded, aged, and armed with a sniper's rifle stands Kevin. Near him are two older women, carrying weapons as well, trained on Pax, writhing on the ground.

And now Eva has her gun in my face again.

"Get down here, bitch."

SIXTH STORY

FATAL FLAW

Eva

EVA

1

PASSION

~

Passion is a slutty, unfaithful bitch. She gets us to do things we would never do, then stabs us in the back with failure. I watch Michael waddle across Caxm with his gun and ammo like a big, limp dick, flaccid in all his power. He makes his way to that old coot who gives him supplies. Does she want him? Is that what her kindness is about, kinky, old succubus.

He gets food and a blanket from her, then lumbers on chasing Fetty or Lupina or whomever else he wants to fuck as Lupina chases Pax, and Fetty chases her devils.

No, passion, you fickle bitch, I won't fall for your tricks. I know I said I would hunt Lupina into the forest on her quest to find Pax. But, no thanks, Lupina, better to let you fall apart on your own as passion pushes you forward on your impossible journey. I have no ill will toward you, I just want to survive and the best way to survive is to be rational.

Rationality is not pushing Lupina into the forest to find Pax. And it certainly isn't driving Fetty to attack the base by herself, crazy-ass chica. If I thought like her, I would have killed her when she charged me and struck up like a slivering snake and knocked me off the horse. Maybe, I should have killed her. When she put her knife against my throat, I saw that at least she gets it. Probably the only one out of all these sniveling babies who gets it: survival of the fittest. And for that, above all, I should have killed my former friend.

Maybe a mistake, but I assume the odds of her making it back from the base alive are nil. No need for me to follow her into the forest either, but maybe I can tilt the odds more in my favor. Yes, very rational, very smart.

I formulate the plan and add layers to it. Not just a warning, but maybe an alliance, then all this can be mine, and I can enjoy the safety and security of being completely in charge. Fetty challenged my leadership when she knocked me off the horse and now, perhaps, I look weak. Better shore up my strength, find out who is on my side, or not. Maybe, I don't need anyone on my side. I am, after all, the only one responsible for my survival, despite that stupid oath with the dirty water.

I walk away from the chapel and head back to my horse, Ringo, the only personality I want to be around right now. Obedient, nice, stoic—more people should be like Ringo. Everyone is watching me with amused looks on their faces as I pet my horse. We'll see who's smiling in a few days. I mount the horse and take my familiar position above everyone else.

Cisco is back with his Mexicans now that he doesn't get to fuck me anymore. He is telling the story of what happened in the chapel and before. He is probably making Fetty out to be some kind of queen. Yes, I need to nip that shit, enact the plan and take control.

The Mexicans are all looking at me on Ringo with surly grins. They are waiting to see if I carry out on my threat to go after Lupina searching for Pax.

Part of me wants to find and kill that snobby twat. I've detested him ever since he once said to me, "Oh, yeah, I forgot you're Jewish." So casually, like it didn't matter. He saw my dark, biracial skin and automatically thought it excluded me from his special club. "You would know I was Jewish if you ever went to Temple," I said to myself at the time.

And now, that prick is the one responsible for killing our savior, the only one who got it, besides me, and maybe, Fetty. Survival of the fittest, by any means necessary. Oh, he/we sold whores into prostitution, BFD. Oh, he got the local militia and our Afghani base to attack each other at the same time, sounds like a genius plan to me. So what if the other teenagers were sacrificed in the shadowplay? If they were strong like us/me, they wouldn't be in that situation.

I stomp through the village with their stares following me while they wonder if I, too, will disappear into the forest to follow the passionate ones who wear their guilt and love on their sleeve like a bunch of suckers.

The LDS look up at me with dubious concern. Spencer, like Cisco, has spread the sermon of the chapel. But I can tell Ezra and others are hoping I plunge into the forest, never to return. No need to have a black leader, I can see it in her eyes and behind her fake face.

Everyone is against me. The LDS, the Mexicans, most of East High is outside of Caxm or not important, I have no one on my side, but that's OK, at least I know where they stand, alone. Friends and followers, too, in a way, are just a more dangerous enemy—nearer to strike—and deserved to be treated as such (except Ringo, of course).

Only one little contingent is unaccounted for, away in the hills, chasing their own twisted little version of passion.

I come up with a good plan, a satisfactory way to satiate the stares of those little scaredy-cats who are doubting if I have enough balls to head into the forest and take on Fetty and Lupina's little group of losers.

I pull the reins and head into the trees. I navigate Ringo through the dense growth and branches until I have to jump down and guide her by hand. We head toward the mountain crest, away from Caxm and all their pitying stares. Then I double back, skirt above the village and back toward the hills, where Annie and Paco trollop with their wild little band of heathens.

I leave Caxm behind, for the moment.

DESPITE THE COWBOY HAT, horse, and rifle, I am no tracker. I can't sniff the fallen leaves, or some shit, and know which way the hunted party traveled. But I can follow sheep droppings. And I've learned enough in my days here that Pax and Annie's herd will prefer mountain meadows to dense forests.

I stay on that path, mainly walking along with Ringo, until I reach a creek adorned with well-chewed grass. I tie up the horse and let her drink from the sullied stream while I go upstream, far enough to find the spring, and drink the clean, pure water.

I sit on a mound of dirt and look out over the valley. My gaze follows the stream downhill to some meadows and small ponds. In the distance, I can see a mass of little clouds slowly moving around the meadow and surrounding forest. In the shade of an outcropping of trees, a large blanket is spread out and covered with a mess of bodies, white, black, and brown, bundled together. No need to hurry. I sit and rest and watch.

Maybe I should just join them, discard my worldly cares and ploys for Caxm. Sitting next to the spring, I think about what path Kevin would take.

The pansexuality and polyamory of their group would have no appeal to him, doesn't really to me either. But the freedom of it, the lack of rules and control, maybe? One thing that people always got wrong about Kevin, about me, for that matter, is that they assumed we always needed to be in control.

People assumed we are control freaks. But Kevin didn't want control, he just hated being controlled. There is a huge difference. Any talk of abuse of authority or stupid, vain rules and his eyes would just gloss-over like he was on some other planet fighting some huge revolution then he would come to and probably do something crazy or worse/better, he would plan something out, long and intricate, to undermine the powers in control.

Annie and Paco's group has the appeal of anarchy. There is no authority, no rules, just freedom in the hills to mind the sheep and do whatever the fuck you want.

I bounce up and retrace my steps back down the stream to Ringo. I mount the saddle and start the downhill slide, half-speed, half-break down toward the pond and meadows. Between the sheep bleats and the siren song of moans, sharp yips break out as the sheepdogs alert them to my approach.

They jump up from their shaded, resting dens and bolt toward me with barks both eager and fearful. I break into a trot and emerge into the meadow as the dogs circle me, and I sooth Ringo. Once calm, I guide her closer to the Annie and Paco's clan.

The view is surreal from atop my high horse. A cuddle puddle of teenagers naked and spread out on a large, thin fabric. They are half-asleep, in a sex, drug, and alcohol induced slumber. They make their own wine from our ground-fallen fruit and rumors abound that they have found a supply of cannabis and opium coming up from Afghanistan.

There are about twelve teenagers sprawled out on a patchwork of blankets. Some have permanently shirked their responsibility to Caxm, some are here just for a break. Danny is with them, his muscular body bookended by two skanky-ass white girls. But I focus on David, the nerdy vintner we adopted from the other barracks after he spied on them for us. He smiles a big grin, happy at his new place, making love to girls and boys who would never give him the time of day back home.

Annie carves out a path through the limbs as she stretches out her muscular, bare body, looking up at me upside down.

"Hey, pretty girl, you finally ready to join us?"

"Tempting," I say. "But I'm just checking in, seeing how you're doing on supplies."

She nimbly pops up and takes the rein of my horse then pets Ringo along her muzzle, nuzzling chin against chin as she receives a big sloppy lick. She pulls back and looks up at me. "You should stay for a bit." She hands me a bottle of fruit wine. I reach down, grab the bottle and take a swig. It tastes like garbage but does the trick.

I hand the bottle back and look at her, then look around at the camp, the sheep, and the teenagers starting to stir. I scan their approaches. I spot a stand of rifles, unattended, against a tree.

I return my gaze to Annie as Paco stands up and embraces her from behind, wrapping his arms around her naked body and kissing her neck while he stares up at me with sexy, fuck me eyes.

"What about safety?" I ask. "I mean, I'm glad you get to have fun and all, but you're not safe here."

Annie tilts her head and looks at me like I'm a child, insane considering all we've been through. "No one is going to attack *us*," she says. "We have nothing of value."

"The sheep. You. Annie, I love you, but it's not safe here."

"That's sweet, sweetie, but we have no enemies. And we have an...arrangement with the local tribes. We are safe."

"Relax, Eva, we are mightier than you think," Paco says from behind his embrace.

"You're too trusting. The sheep belong to Caxm too. Speaking of, you can delay the next delivery by a week or so. A bunch of people took off on a crazy mission, so fewer mouths to feed."

"What?" Annie asks, bothered by the order thrown at her. "Who, what?"

"It's about Pax and Kevin, new information, shit that happened during the Battle of the Base, and after. A bunch of our friends from East, Lupina, Michael, Fetty, took off, probably won't be back for a while, so you can hang back."

"What did they find out?" she asks, and it actually looks like she cares, like she feels guilty for not being part of their expedition. I need to keep that curiosity down.

"Not much...Lupina is eager to find anything about Pax. No worries, though, I let you know of any news."

I pull the reins and tug my horse away from their petting and head back toward the forest. Then I stop, maneuver Ringo back around. "Oh, and David, get dressed, you're coming with me."

The others just snicker at my demand, but David meets my stare. I raise my eyebrows, and he sits up, gathers his stuff while covering his manhood.

2

THE WATCHER

～

"Y ou wanna walk or ride bitch?" I ask David as we disappear into the forest, followed by the dogs and laughs from Annie's clan.

"I'll walk," he says, humiliated. "Just carry my stuff." He lops his backpack behind the saddle and reaches up to attach the straps.

We keep trotting and our pace makes him skip and side-walk as he jumps up over and over to make the connection. His glasses start to fall from his face, and he stops, uber-protective of his only pair of spectacles.

"Stop!" he whines.

I rein the horse in and wait for David to fasten his pack. I look back at him. His pale skin seems to be finally clear of blemishes on our natural diet and time in the sun. His mouse-colored hair is still greasy but seems manlier, more rebellious. He could almost be a Kevin if he wasn't such a pussy.

He finishes with the pack then walks up to the front of the horse and takes the lead. He guides us through the branches and bushes to a worn trail. The dogs abandon us to go back to the sheep.

"I assume Pax and Kevin didn't make it back."

"No, according to Fetty, Pax killed Kevin."

"Well, that's good—"

I rip the rein from David's hand and try to snap his head with it, but he is too short.

"—It's not good that Kevin is dead."

"…I mean for us, one less person that knows."

"They know."

"What do they know?" he asks without looking back.

"They know we sold the girls."

David shakes his head. "What else do they know? Do they know I planted cell phones in our barracks for Kevin?"

"They wouldn't really care about *those* cell phones."

"Do they know I was watching the girls in the major's room when you all had the meeting with Kevin?"

"No, they don't know that. But Fetty may figure it out."

David halts to face me, puts up his hand to stop Ringo, but she keeps walking.

"If they don't know about me, then why the fuck am I coming with you? I'm not in trouble."

"*I* know what you did. That's why you're coming with me. Now hurry up. We got shit to do before we lose control of the situation."

THE NEXT DAY we slide back into Caxm to gauge the mood and to weapon up. Everyone ignores us and goes about their tasks like I don't matter. They don't even flash the "I told you so" smiles, and worse, nobody comes up to ask if I was successful, if I found Fetty or Lupina and Pax. They all assume I failed. I tie up Ringo next to Cisco's horse, Vaquero.

The Mexicans start to gather when David loads up a Humvee. Cisco comes up to us as I fire it up. He puts his hand up to stop me as drive by, but my only response is my middle finger.

I half expect him to jump in the other Humvee, the one abandoned by Michael, and chase after. Give me some lecture about how I can't take Caxm property without approval, but he just shakes his head. Too bad he only thinks he lost a Humvee and not the village. Stupid, weak boy. He couldn't stop me, anyway. HE only one who can stop me is on her way to an impossible mission that I will make even more dangerous.

With David at the turret, I head down the road, back to the base and the first step in my plan to be in complete control of my destiny.

THE BASE LOOKS different as we approach, devoid of civilization, like an ancient archeological site with tribal totems and lingering smoke. The gun towers are occupied and so is the front gate. We are immediately met by guards and a cavalcade of Humvees coming from the motor pool.

Unlike our previous National Guard overlords, these soldiers expect an attack and probably have thwarted their share. I stop our Humvee and can almost feel the quivers of David raising his hands in surrender from above.

I, too, put my hands up and slowly start to exit the vehicle while in their gunsights. All of sudden, I feel tremendous fear. Being rich, with a Jewish American Princess mother, I sometimes forget how other people outside of my community see me. In the diverse neighborhoods of east Denver, I was adept at sliding back and forth between worlds, black, white, Jewish, Christian, southern, urban. My biracial skin and curly hair even awoke a new, celebrity-like status in the past few years. I was super-sexy, cool.

But, under their fearsome guns, I am not cool; I am an other. I am a black person to be suppressed by fear and authority. When Jaden and Michael told the story of being harassed by the police, at first, I thought they were lying. That their white parent automatically gave them a pass to what we see all the time in the news. But, of course, that was naïve. I know that now as they fretfully bark orders at me to exit the vehicle with hands up. I keep my face stern, my mouth closed, to cover the braces that make me seem juvenile.

Cool or white is not how good these old boys see me. Not that telling them I am Jewish would belie their hate and fear. I feel the need to acquiesce the leadership of this mission to lily-white David, but he is too full of fear as well.

"Get down on your knees!" A petulant soldier yells at me. I don't want to submit; I don't want to show weakness. I wish for muscular Michael up on the .50 caliber and clever Kevin doing the talking, but I must be strong.

"We are here to make peace," I stay, still standing up, but this does not make me feel strong.

"You are about to be attacked," I continue while throwing a fake scared look into the forest, and this seems to pique their interest. "Soon."

They escort us inside the gate while keeping a skittish watch on the trees. They seem to be scared of the forest, like a bogeyman haunts it, terrorizing them from the shadows.

OUR HUMVEE HAS BEEN SEARCHED but sits abandoned outside the gate. Our weapons taken, we stand surrounded by soldiers but at least their guns no longer point at us. They stand stoic, but pay more attention to the forest than David and I. They seem to think that I might be a diversion to an impending attack. [1]

It seems ridiculous to describe an attack by one teenage girl, but this is the coin I used to gain entry. But what if Michael was making the hunting of men up about Fetty? And she agreed just to scare us and justify her prowess.

"Someone is coming to attack the base," I start, vaguely hoping I can lead into the kicker. "She is coming in from the forest." I point to the trees, to their dread, and start to feel confident that I can barter an alliance based on their fear.

But they actually laugh at me. "Ha. One person, a girl is coming to attack us?"

I look the fool. I decide to take a chance, to paradoxically put my trust in the words of the friends I am about to betray.

"Yes, the same one person, one girl, who has been hunting you and all your friends in the forest. You know. You know when your friends don't come back, or when one of you gets picked off, you know you aren't facing an army or militia," I say. They look captivated so I decide to hammer the point with a hidden truth. "She is the one that blew up…that fracked your leader…she snuck in the other night, knocked him out, and left two grenades as a gift. This one *girl*…has been hunting you, and now she is on the way here to kill you all."

They are no longer laughing. I have them in the palm of my hand.

"You're facing a skinny Ethiopian girl," I say. I take off my hat and point to my kinky hair. I point to my face. "Smaller than me, but looks similar."

"Why are you telling us this?"

"She's crazy. She attacked me. She has a bloodlust. And, I need your help. We have a village, an orchard with fresh fruit, fields, and sheep, a sustainable food source. But I need your help controlling it, and we will trade back and forth. Information, food, supplies. Deal?"

Some of the soldiers laugh again, but a tall man with a big, blond beard steps forward. "Quiet! You four." He points with his bushy chin. "Head into the forest. Split up into teams of two. One group will patrol approaches; the other starts hunting deeper in."

"No fucking way, man. We don't go into the forest anymore."

"You go into the forest or we drop you right now."

A slight smile escapes my lips at their timidity. They are so scared of the forest; is it because of Fetty's hunting? They seem to be weighing their options. Then I realize the truth through a lie.

Fetty told us she fracked the leader because she figured that the hunting game in the forest would eventually catch up to her. But that wasn't true. *We don't go into the forest anymore.* Fetty snuck into the base and fracked the leader because she had no one else to hunt.

The trepidation of the soldiers and the prowess of Fetty starts to gnaw at me; maybe, I chose the wrong horse to bet on. But this is my lot, and maybe I can help them along.

"You know," I say. "If she's coming for you, and doesn't expect you to be out in the forest, you're not much safer on the base."

They look at me with resentment, at my confidence, my challenges to their manliness. I know, at that moment, if they didn't need me, if they weren't so scared, they probably would have shot me down.

"Get the fuck out of here," their leader tells them.

3

CUTTHROAT

~

Scared of playing adult, timid to the fights and tension, David forsakes the .50 caliber and sits in the Humvee next to me, like a child who wants to be close to mommy. Nervous, as usual, he breaks open the conversation with worry. "What if they turn on us?" he asks.

A fair question, but in many ways the "soldiers" in the Humvees behind us are just as scared as David. Left alone, with no material or logistical support from home, they are probably deathly aware that their food supply is limited.

"They need us, and they're scared," I say. And after saying it out loud, I realize the big blond leader and the others in the Humvees following us are probably the most chicken of the bunch; I suspect they jumped into the Humvees to avoid Fetty.

"Yeah, um, but all the more reason for them to take control. Right, isn't that why...what you're doing?

"I'm not doing this because I'm scared," I snap. "I'm doing this because I'm smart."

My frustration comes out on the gas pedal, and I start burning around corners and hitting the bumps, jostling David all around.

I finally slow down to let the other vehicles catch up. "And besides, as long as there are groups of us outside of Caxm, like Annie and Paco, like Michael and Fetty, the soldiers from the base will never have complete control."

"But those groups aren't on your side either."

"And the militia and the base weren't on our side either, but Kevin got them to attack each other, and they're both weaker because of it. A game of cutthroat, it's just a simple game of cutthroat."

"Sounds dangerous."

"Dangerous times, David."

HOURS LATER, we see the sign Jaden and Seth made for Caxm, and I decide to do what Kevin would do, just motor on in with all the Humvees, no introduction, no warning. If they decide to start shooting each other, oh well, just more of my enemies reduced.

Cisco and Spencer lead the troops out, guns ready for a fight, but they don't stand a chance against the .50 calibers, and they know it.

I exit the Humvee all nonchalant.

"What the fuck did you do?" Cisco yells at me.

"What? We needed help, trading partners."

I look back over my shoulder at the soldiers in the Humvees. They look scared, and maybe, David is right; their fear isn't necessarily a good thing.

I raise my hands. "Everyone, calm down. We can work together."

"No fucking way," Cisco says.

"You...you shouldn't have done this, Eva, you should have asked first," Spencer says.

"Look, you wouldn't have approved, and Fetty was out there

killing men, killing these soldiers on our behalf, without our permission, and I want the violence to end. I want to make peace."

Felicia walks up, bold with her baby slung around her chest and her rifle in her hands. "Eva," she says. "I thought Fetty was your friend?"

This stings. I want to just go back to the Humvees, climb on board and tell all of Caxm to lay down their arms or we'll open fire.

But I look at Felicia's worn, tired face. I look at the hair of Hector, Jr. poking up under her chin, and feel I don't have the heart for this. Maybe I should have just joined Annie and Paco in their beautiful debauchery.

Regardless, I am here now. "What did Lupina say? What is Caxm founded on? Sharing. That's what *caxm* means in Tajiki, right? There is no reason why we can't all just get along."

Out of the shadows, quietly, Seth has climbed up on my Humvee and taken control of the .50 caliber David abandoned.

"We also named this village after my twin brother, Sam, who these people, your new friends, killed."

I turn and stare Seth down, look at his angry face behind the .50 caliber.

"Put your weapons down," I command. I turn back around and look at the others, Felicia, Cisco, Spencer. "All of you, put your weapons down or they will open fire and kill every one of you. Every. Last. One," I say, staring right at Felicia and her baby.
*1

Felicia gives me a hate stare that could melt metal and just turns around, rifle, baby, and all, and begins walking away. Yesenia joins her, but when Cisco takes a step in that direction I fire my rifle near his feet.

I hear the metal on metal scrapes of the guns behind me being moved into position on the Humvees. Seth has me dead to rights, but is he willing to kill all his friends on behalf of his dead brother? A shot has been fired, my warning across the bow. Everyone freezes, stares at me and then up at the big guns behind me, staring down at them. I know by the fearful looks on Felicia, Spencer, and everyone's faces that they will surrender their weapons.

I walk over to David. "Collect their weapons. And next time, stay in the turret."

Next, I walk up to Seth. I continue the poker face. The thing about passion, about love, and other weak emotions: it's leverage. Unlike me, he loves the tribe more than he loves being in control. But his big gun is still aimed straight at me.

"Well, what's it going to be? Should we start the killing? You can start with me. They wouldn't mind."

For a brief second, I think he is going to fire, that the death of his twin brother introduced enough chaos for him not to give a fuck. But he only bends down, like a cat getting ready to pounce, and launches himself, sideways, with a weird, twisting flip out of the Humvee. He lands it, then disappears under the orchard and off into the forest. Too quick, and too spastic for me to fire on.

I turn back around to Caxm and David, staring at the scene. "David...get to work."

ANYONE CAN LEAD as long as people are fed and safe. It's been a couple of weeks since the soldiers and I came in and took the guns. Not much has changed. The residents of Caxm grumbled and complained but went back to work.

The LDS group was the first to comply. The next day, after meeting in their chapel, they went back to the fields and their newly constructed beehives without prompting. The Mexicans soon followed and then everyone went back to work. Even the older villagers seemed to shrug off the changing of the guard.

Honestly, it feels like most of Caxm was glad to surrender their weapons and the responsibility, trauma, and guilt they bring. They shed their guns like a bad cold and became more productive because of it.

More so, because, essentially nothing else changed. We were

not setting up new rules; we were not burning people at the stake or whipping people at a flagpole or barking stupid, egotistical orders. Knowing how much I hate to be controlled, I had no desire to subject anyone else to a heavy-handed authority.

But I could tell that they didn't give up all hope of overturning our rule. They, just like most weak people, placed their hope in others. They frequently looked to the forest and hills with a longing for some heroes, Fetty, Lupina and Pax, Annie and Paco, to sweep in and save them. Let somebody else get their hands dirty. It's just basic risk-benefit analysis. As long as you're being fed, as long as you're safe, why in the world would you risk your life if your life is not in danger?

Even the soldiers soon folded into the routine. After a couple of days, I expected them to send a party back to the base, to round up their comrades, maybe even gather some teenagers who survived. I was worried that we could increase the population of Caxm beyond our ability to support. I was preparing arguments, orders, tactics to persuade the soldiers to limit the number of those who could come into Caxm, or at the very least, pay for it with MREs, supplies, and equipment.

But they never left. They never broached the topic. After a while, I could tell that they didn't want to go back, even for resupply. I thought it might because of Fetty. Maybe they so feared the bogeywoman terror she instilled that they had no desire to take a chance, to risk safety for camaraderie. But it wasn't just fear and food that kept the soldiers in Caxm. It was guilt. I could sense they didn't want to go back to the base; they wanted to cut that time out of their life, because they wanted to bury their sins. But sins, no matter how dead and rotted in the ground, always have a way of coming back to life.

4

A DEAD GIRL OR A LIVE BOY
A DEAD BOY OR A LIVE GIRL?

~

Last year, when I was still a high school cheerleader and still best friends with Annie and Fetty, I went through a terrible time. I was pregnant, and I decided to go to the women's clinic alone. I could have gone with Annie; lord knows she would have supported my decision. Even Fetty, so engaged in her family's Orthodox Christianity, would have silently sat by my side. Or my liberal mother, too, would have relished using the situation as a teaching moment, a crucial pinnacle of her struggle for the right to choose.

I was always comfortable with being uncomfortable, a stealthy wraith who could move between worlds effortlessly, so I thought this decision would be easier. That going alone would be no big deal.

I told no one, not even the father. I went to the clinic and filled out their forms with a clinical detachment contrasting the turmoil going on within me, only semi-excited that they had multiracial as a selection under race. But why did I feel so conflicted about the abortion? I was raised in a liberal family, in a liberal neighborhood. Even my father's family, esteemed Southern Baptists from the South, would have understood. They fought for liberal rights, too, until the Jim Crow and gerrymandering was too much of a stifling oppression, and they took their money and pride elsewhere, unable to defeat entrenched white politicians that won no matter what faults they carried.

I felt a huge animosity toward the prevalence of anti-choice propaganda in media and culture, and the disgusting billboards that made me feel somewhat bad about my choice. Were they creeping into my mind and making feel guilty? Not only did they want to control my body, but my mind as well. Or maybe it was the potentiality of a child growing in my body. But there are literally billions of potentialities of a child growing within a man's balls. Hell, I used to think, every year uber-Christian (and hot) Tim Tebow doesn't get married and procreate, scores of potential children were being aborted.

Or maybe it was just nerves, and my bizarre decision to face it alone. To shun my family and friends who would have welcomed the chance to care for me. But I felt some guilt and trepidation at the decision.

Unnaturally guilt-ridden, I remember sitting in the waiting room, staring at a picture of my driver's license that I just received back from the nurse checking me in. I was focused on my picture on the ID. I looked like a girl and a woman at the same time. Framed in the official document, proof of my growing up, my changing face seemed like that of an adult, but my suppressed smile, covering the braces underneath, my big, innocent eyes, still carried the aura of a little girl shining through.

This girl-woman pictured on the piece of plastic was making a difficult, emotional decision, by herself. But I resolved to do it alone, to keep it my little secret, safe from the possibility of stupid judgments by anyone, or any gross, scalding billboard of shame looming over me in the present or future.

My pensive stare stayed focused on my heart. A small, black heart resting below my left shoulder on the picture. A symbol, an indication, that I was an organ donor. If I died, the state could carve up my body and distribute my organs to people in desperate need of a transplant.

I gave them permission to use my body. I remember chuckling about this at the time, a too loud, awkward laugh that rolled through the somber clinic. I couldn't stop giggling, to the point where the nice nurse whispered with an accent similar to relatives in my father's family, "Dear, are you OK?"

I stopped laughing and looked up at her. "A dead boy or a live girl...or a live girl or a dead boy, which is it?"

She only pursed her lips and shook her head, confused, but also recognizing the southern saying I was trying to express. She muttered "A dead girl..." and clumsily went back to her paperwork.

See, while looking at my little black heart under my official, non-smiling girl to woman portrait, I couldn't help but find the humor in the value many conservatives put on me. If the boy who got me pregnant was dead, and had a good liver that someone needed, even if the possible transplant would result in the imminent saving of another person's life, they still needed his pre-given permission to have access to his body, his *dead* body. But, of course, I was a live girl with a "baby" inside, and they felt they didn't need my permission to my body. So, from their perspective, a live girl had less control over their body than a dead boy.

I SIT on Michael's abandoned Humvee and flick the useless driver's license under my chin, a snap of the ancient relic, a vestige from a previous life where a government tried to regulate what we did behind the wheel of a vehicle or under the bright lights of a doctor's office.

I look up from my little black organ donor heart, and inspect

Caxm. It's been weeks since I took over and no man has control over my body or mind.

But that was all before I thought I saw a dead boy. Hungry and weak, like a neglected dog, Seth came back into Caxm shepherding a group of people like some hard-earned prize. At first, I thought he found Lupina's party or stumbled on Paco and Annie's herd and convinced them to give up the life of hedonism for the chance to bring me down.

I see two women bookending Seth. They are older, probably in their late twenties or early thirties. They seem experienced, tough with their worn gear and rifles and stoic stares. One is tall and skinny, boyish with short hair and pale skin. The other is shorter, curvy with dark skin and kind, South Asian features.

But what freezes everyone in their tracks, gets jaws to drop, and even little whimpers to slip, is the other person Seth parades along. He wears a goofy bucket hat, and is older looking, with a long, wispy beard. He has the same dark, penetrating eyes as Kevin. He walks like Kevin, the awkward, spastic gait ready to spring off at any second, in any direction, a walk both tired and energetic at the same time. He even looks spastic while pushing along a black bike, muddied and overloaded with gear. His gaze quickly scans and deciphers the setting like a robot reading images, stats, and trajectories that we can't see.

His scan follows Seth's pointing finger and settles on me; sizing me up, he moves his left hand from the bike grip to a black, futuristic sniper rifle fastened to the handlebars of the bike. He leans forward and thrusts the bike toward me. I focus on a crucifix hanging down and swinging from his neck, the beads shifting and shining in the morning light. I don't want to look at his piercing gaze, the judgment and wrath that may come from Kevin for betraying our tribe to the base. But the cross seems like an odd choice for Kevin, who is such a tortured existentialist and raging atheist. Did he find God in the wilderness? Forgiveness?

He stops right in front of me and stands up straight, the cross bounces and settles on his chest, his face shadowed under a bucket hat and fruit trees. The crowd, the armed soldiers on my side, are motionless, staring at Kevin staring at me. We are all dumbstruck.

"Where is he?"

"Who?" I respond. Is he asking about Pax?

"Kevin! Seth said you would know. I've travelled thousands of miles through hell to bring my son his medicine. Where the fuck is he?"

5

THE GOSPEL OF MARK

~

After awkward introductions, I shepherd a small group into the LDS chapel. We gather around, calm and quiet but full of tension on the benches in a sloppy square. I allowed Spencer, Cisco, and Seth to join us from Caxm, and they sit on one bench. On another bench squats the bearded soldier and two of his lieutenants.

Opposite them sit Mark and the two young women, Joni and Spriha. The females rest patient and silent, but Mark is on edge and refuses to put down his rifle. Similar to Fetty, he holds it close like a security blanket.

It's freaky, looking at him; he looks so much like Kevin and carries the same dangerousness, a presence both alluring and foreboding.

Next to me sits David, smart but useless, and I feel outnumbered and despised. I can easily lose control of if I'm not careful.

"Where is Kevin?" Mark repeats, calm and cold.

"I'm sorry to do this to you, Mark; I will say what needs to be said, but there is information we need from you that I'm afraid we won't get if we jump into the story of Pax and Kevin."

"Are they OK? Just tell me that."

I do the lip press, head shake denial thing as the soldier-leader steps in, "What is going on in America? How did you get here?"

Mark's dark-circled eyes squint, so similar to Kevin's, with their perceptiveness and behind the curtain calculations. He is running scenarios now and probably realizing it wouldn't be efficient to force the truth out of us. He takes a resigned breath and starts his story.

"AMERICA IS both hell and purgatory at the same time," he says, then pauses wondering where to go from such a broad statement. He starts caressing the crucifix while building the story in his head. The beads lay across his rifle and some seem to have hard scars, marked into their round little spheres. I recognize the necklace I was so fixated on. It was the same one Todd, Kevin's dear friend in the wheelchair, carried around, always laying in his left hand while he repeatedly worked the beads through his fingers.

"Is Todd OK?" I ask. I am being both sincere and wanting to show a display of empathy—walking that strange tightrope that only women have to walk—the demonstration of practicality and sincerity at the same time.

"I was in the mountains when it happened. I didn't know until a few days later because I was deep in the backcountry. But I saw jets continuously scrambling and saw the ash descend. I rushed to my Jeep, then back to Denver, and it was deserted, so strange; I grew up in that city, saw it grow from a cow town to a sprawling metropolis, and it was practically empty. Yes, there was ash, but we've had bigger snowstorms in May. And almost everyone was gone.

"I WENT to my house and no Kevin. So, I went to Sally, uh,

Todd's mom...I went to their house. Media was silent or just repeated the same meaningless message. She filled me in about the evacuation, with teenagers leaving first followed by the chaos of everyone escaping Denver soon after, but the city wasn't destroyed or uninhabitable, just covered in a dusting of ash.

"Todd was with her, of course. He couldn't be part of the evacuation, and she couldn't leave him. She begged me...begged me to stay and help take care of Todd, to help provide, to fend off the wolves she knew would eventually come. But I only stayed for a couple of days. I broke into a pharmacy to steal as much medicine as she needed and to gather a large supply of Kevin's epilepsy prescription. Then I left. I told her my son came first, and I left. Todd understood. He gave me a smile and his rosary to keep me safe, to guide me. Then he loaded an encrypted communication program on my phone that he developed with Kevin."

"Does it work?" Blond beard asks. "Can we call America?"

All the other benches throw him a scowl, but Mark just responds. "No, it doesn't work like that. I can only post encrypted messages, like a message board, to other cell phones that have the program and keys, and it communicates through Bluetooth, requiring a network of programmed phones to come in close contact to spread, so the distribution is very slow.

"The last message from Sally and Todd was from a few weeks ago, when I met Joni and Spriha in Syria. We all were sneaking through at night, taking advantage of the chaos, and decided to travel together."

Everyone leans in, fascinated by the pending adventure story, but Mark and his silent sirens just look at us with blank faces. His jaw clenches and that piercing Kevin stare returns.

"Look," he says while leaning in and running the beads through his fingers like Todd used to do. "It's cute that you all like story time, but I'm not going to relive that shit for your entertainment. Hey! Look at me, you shifty-eyed motherfuckers...I *will* tell you this...." He holds up Todd's beads. "These marks...these notches on the beads, they are for each person I had to kill to get here, to get to Kevin. I have filled up over two decades so far, twenty-three marks, twenty-three total kills."

He drops the crucifix, and it bounces with a clink off his rifle, now clutched in both hands. He scans each bench, each face focused on his words. "And I'll fill up this goddamn rosary right now, mark off another decade, if you don't tell me what the hell happened to my son."

I REMAIN calm under his threat but look around at all the scared faces, on all the benches, and tally up what everyone knows or doesn't know. Cisco and Spencer were in this chapel when Fetty spun her story. They heard Fetty say that the leader said Pax killed Kevin for selling those girls into slavery. The soldiers were at the base after and chased Pax and Kevin through the forest. Maybe, they saw or came up on Kevin's murder.

Do we know for sure that Kevin is dead? Seeing Mark, thinking he was Kevin, rekindled my hope that he was still alive, and, I just feel pity for Mark; I can't imagine a parent's struggle, their long epic journey to save a child only to find out this news.

I want to give him false hope. And it's not because I am scared of being another mark on Todd's necklace. I want to do the smart, rational thing here, and truthfully, like his son, Mark is another unstable variable, too uncertain and dangerous in his actions to be kept around. Now that I am in charge, my perspective of instability has changed.

Everyone else seems scared; they don't want to break the bad news. Now, they look to me to be the leader. So be it.

"Pax and Kevin disappeared into the wilderness months ago, and haven't been seen since."

"Why," he asks.

A few spectators look shocked at my half-lie, but I continue.

"I don't know why. They had issues. Michael, Jaden, Lupina, and Charlotte went to go find them, and they haven't returned either, but knock yourself out. You seem to be apt at the whole wilderness thing."

I FEEL WEIRD, ashamed, uneasy at the brashness of my tone with Mark. I don't know if the guilt stems from him finding out his son is missing (and probably dead). I don't know if it is because he is an adult, and I am a teenager. I don't know if it is some fucked up cultural thing where a female, a black female, shouldn't be bold and rude to an older, white male. I don't know why I want to make amends, especially after he threatened to kill me. Maybe it's just that I miss Kevin too. But after our wonderful pep talk in the chapel, I walk over to Mark to seek some kind of peace.

We are outside, and he is going through his gear with a determined efficiency similar to Kevin, unloading the bags on his bike, emptying and organizing his backpack. At the uncomfortableness of the situation I bring Ringo with me to break the ice. Everyone loves a horse, and she is my safe space.

"My girl wanted to meet your girl," I say, awkward and almost fawning. When he looks up, confused, I nod to his bike.

"Oh, yeah. This is Bucephalus. Kevin and I built her."

"She is quite a ride."

Mark ignores this and ignores Ringo, too. He starts uncoupling big batteries from the bike.

"I need to charge the batteries. You have a generator. You cool with me using it? I assume you are the one I should ask."

"Sure. You going to look for Kevin?"

Mark doesn't answer, just gives me a no shit look that goes right through me, like he knows I am just trying to get rid of him, like he knows I am hiding something.

"Joni and Spriha are going to stay here. They've had a hard road, and this isn't their fight."

"That's fine," I say but realize he wasn't really asking.

"And we'll be communicating by radio. If anything comes up we can get a hold of each other."

Was that another threat? Kevin was always so cold and calculating but relatively sweet with me. It's disarming to be on the other side of their killer intensity, the eyes and thoughts that just bore right through you.

I meet his stare and challenge his bluff, his suspecting me of lying and leaving his companions here to keep tabs.

"So, I didn't want to say anything in front of the group, because not everyone knows, and we don't know for sure. But, according to the soldiers from the base…" Am I really going to say this? What was I thinking?

"What? Enough pussyfooting, Eva. You need to tell me what happened to Kevin."

"I don't know the full truth—"

"Tell me what you know."

"Pax and Kevin…they weren't getting along. Pax was unstable, not dealing well with the violence…oh, yeah, we killed the National Guard soldiers after they whipped Michael. Kevin led the attack."

"Is that why you aren't on the base? When I left the States, I was able to get the coordinates, but when we ran into Seth on the way there, he said you moved. He seemed upset about what happened and wouldn't talk about it."

"Yeah, well, he lost his twin brother in the fighting. You can say it's been a hard road for us too. And Pax wasn't handling it well. He was aggressive with Kevin…with some of the stuff we had to do to survive. During our escape to this village, they got in an argument and took off into the woods. Pax said something about the soldiers we fought on the road were actually kids, other teenagers like us, and Kevin didn't believe him. Pax took Kevin to show him; they never came back."

"This isn't really news, Eva."

"Yeah, well, according to some soldiers from the base, they said…they said that they saw Pax kill Kevin."

Mark just continues to stare at me, jaw clenched, gaze burning. "Pax killed Kevin?"

"Yeah. That's the story."

"And you heard this from the soldiers that you fought on the base."

"On the road. The ones we fought on the base are all dead."

"But they're on the same side, those soldiers? They are all part of the coup?"

I nod.

"And you invited them into this base, and that's why all the teenagers hate you?"

I am shocked into silence. Just like Kevin, Mark saw right through me. I start to stammer.

"Look, I appreciate all you've been through, probably makes you think you are stronger and smarter than you are, but I'm going to get a good night's sleep, recharge Bucephalus' batteries, steal some of your abundant food, and then I am going to find my son."

"Sure thing, boss. Just look out for Pax and the others while you're out there."

"Don't play cutthroat with me, little girl; I told you once, I will kill all parties involved, including you."

6

THE WEIGHTED AVERAGE

~

A fter Fetty attacked me, I felt panic, a stricken, primal fear to reach out for more protection. So I went to the base and made an uneasy alliance. I felt safer after, taking control, and safer still when Caxm fell in line with the new order. But that was over a month ago and everything just returned to a numb sort of normalcy, until Mark and his women showed up.

With Mark's arrival, with the discussion about Fetty and Michael and their group, and the morbid mentions of Kevin and Pax, the sun sets to an uneasy feeling. We can feel the tension, the calm before the storm. Even though we have heard nothing from the ones who left, a new danger lurks in the air, palpable and pressuring. I remember reading about how tidal waves empty the beaches, suck out the water before they strike, and this is what it feels like.

A premonition tells me to sleep in one of the Humvees, hidden under a cave of branches woven together in false fasces protection; the safety of the shelter Michael haunted for many months before he left. I even loaded a go-pack of supplies and food in case I need to leave. But now I sit in his Humvee and wait, wondering about him, us, how we became enemies; not just Michael and I but all of our groups.

When I first met Michael, I really looked up to him. Here was a super smart black kid who had the world under his bright smile. I heard he forsake sports, and I admired him for that. I wanted him to be part of our group, Annie, Fetty and I, and even our jock boy acolytes. He had an alluring presence; Michael was an elite, strong, smart, beautiful; he could have been our valedictorian, and part of me wanted him to be at the top of the class even though I was aiming for the same throne. Part of me wanted a black male, a biracial male to give that speech. After all that happened in our society, from Trevon Martin to Colin Kaepernick, he, we, they, deserved to hear that speech.

But despite his perfect AP scores, despite his straight A's, Michael chose a different route. See, Michael loved theater, loved being on stage. And he was good at it, but it was still a stupid choice. Because the way grades work for the elite, the weighted average of the honor courses get scored higher than electives like theater, orchestra, and strength and conditioning. An A in soft elective counts less toward the GPA than an A in an honors course. So Michael made choice to give up being valedictorian to specialize in theater, to follow a narcissistic path on stage with the other losers in his group: Jaden, Charlotte, Pax, and Lupina. That's how they all became friends, an alliance of averageness and mediocrity.

And he made a choice to follow those losers into the forest. But when I hear their burst of gunfire, when I hear the deafening din of the grenades, I know they returned to fight it out for Caxm. A killer urgency fills the air, efficient and lethal, that sounds tell me Fetty is with them, leading the attack with her killer instinct. Once attacked, you never forget a predator's scent. But Michael will make his way back to the comfort of the cave he spent so many months hiding in, taking the safe, comfortable route of not being the top of his class.

I see him timidly approach the vehicles, carrying a rifle but missing the big one he took. He is looking for another .50 caliber, a weak, pathetic scan unworthy of the big, powerful guns he couldn't even keep.

He doesn't see me in the backseat, lurking. He looks for the other gun, looks for any danger outside his cave. He crawls up on top of the turret, and I sneak out and around.

Two soldiers see him too, they are stalking up, ready to pounce but I wave them off and pop up with my gun on him.

"Don't fucking move, Michael."

SOON AFTER, Michael looks shocked. Pax killed the soldiers, then Mark came in, and Pax and Michael now resemble a couple of toddlers. Pax is thrashing around on the ground, calling out for Lupina over and over like a kid throwing a temper tantrum in front of their mom.

Michael is slack jawed; a tiny spiral of spit drools out of his mouth, hangs there in the moonlight and drops. He has climbed down off the Humvee slow and timid, looking back and forth between Mark and me.

Obviously, they are making the same mistake we all made. Confusing Mark for Kevin, the father for the son. Michael focuses on Mark. He steps forward closer to the father. His eyes narrows on Mark's presence, his cold, omniscient stare mixed with the face of a broken man with nothing to lose.

"Careful," I say.

Michael's big brain starts running the different scenarios. He stepped toward Mark because he thought he was Kevin, thought that his best friend had come back and would lead and save him, save them all. But he makes calculations. Runs the threads to their conclusion. Kevin is dead, and Mark is here to collect on their sins.

From the ground, Pax focuses on Michael, towering over him but still just staring at Mark.

"Am I crazy?" Pax asks in a voice weak and trembling, a soft whisper more chilling than his calls for Lupina. "Am I crazy, Michael?"

"No, you're not crazy, Pax. But you're done. We're all done."

7

A LIFE WORTH LIVING

A LIFE WORTH TAKING

～

E very free weekend, without fail, I would spend my spare time at an equestrian therapy ranch in the foothills northwest of Denver. Living in the city, I always dreamed of owning my own horse, but despite having money, despite living in a relatively large house on a large lot, having a horse in the city was never going to happen. Ironically, our old house had a large detached garage that sat across the alley from an old, large carriage house, specifically built to hold carts and horses.

But now, in the modern era of automobiles, old barns and carriage houses were turned into garages, storage sheds, and sometimes homes, and the only horses in the city were cruelly pulling lovers and tourists in velvet lined carriages through Downtown Denver.

When, as a headstrong and precocious child, horrorstruck and overdramatic at the news that Daddy couldn't buy me a pony, I researched, on my own, the rules and regulations to get a horse and even promised I would pay the annual fee to get a permit. But, notwithstanding the initiative and maturity I showed, my parents wouldn't commit to getting a large animal whose lifespan covers a few decades.

We could have bought a horse and boarded it outside the city, a decent second place prize, I felt. When I found this out, I tried even more clever tactics. I pretended I was scared, snuck into my parent's bed, then feigning a deep slumber, I talked in my sleep, moaning over and over, my imaginary horse's name, Ringo (number one, I guess). When this didn't work, I displayed a multi-day depression episode splattered with quips about suicide and a life not worth living.

As a compromise, my mom sat me down one Sunday morning with a stack of pamphlets. They had pictures of horses on them so, on the inside, I was brimming with delight. I won. My clever antics were going to produce a very special horse of my own.

But the pamphlets weren't an audition sheet for me to make my equine selection. They were for a charity. In the photos, horses roamed and frolicked with the mountains in the background, but pictures in the foreground showed kids and adults with helmets, some in wheelchairs, some being lifted up on harnesses, or strapped and guided on horses by tender caretakers.

As a child, I couldn't reconcile the glorious pictures of roaming horses in a mountain setting with the disabled people attached to them. This is not what I had in mind.

"So, I talked with your father," my mom said, always a bad start to a conversation. "And we agreed that while we appreciate your initiative to have a horse, we just aren't ready or willing for that kind of commitment."

"But Mom—"

"Eva, let me finish. What we did find is this great organization where you can volunteer. You get to learn about horses, how to take care of them, how to clean up after them, how they behave. And maybe…"

And maybe, those words always led to good things. Maybe I get to work for my horse, totally doable.

"…down the road…"

Yes!

"…they will let you ride their horses in your spare time."

I deadpanned a bullshit look at her. "I get to ride their horses.
…"

"Well, yeah, sweetie, it's the best of both worlds. You get to
ride horses, and we don't have to spend thirty years paying for it."

I gave my audible sigh and glanced down at the pamphlet.

I spent hundreds of hours at the therapy ranch. Helping
others, helping myself become a better person. Yay! But most of
all, I got to be close to horses. I connected with them and understood how they connected with different types of people.

I learned to love working with the disabled kids and adults.
The joy horses brought them was shared. The kids with Down
syndrome were the best, a contagious happiness that followed and
spread from them to other humans and horses alike.

But I remember one kid, an older kid, older than I was at the
time. He was big, maybe 200 pounds, and needed to be pushed in
a wheelchair to get around. His parents dropped him off for a few
of hours of respite every other week. They looked drained, almost
broken, with the lifelong burden of supporting their son (and my
mom complained about the obligations for owning a horse). The
boy, Scooter, would freak out every time they left and every time
they came back. Drool leaking from his big head, he would repeat
the same phrases over and over, "Born to be wild, born to be wild.
Scraps for Scooter, scraps for Scooter."

He was emotionally gone; he was mentally gone; he was physically gone. And I couldn't help but think, as I was helping change
his diaper, that maybe it wasn't a life worth living.

Does that make me a bad person? Am I telling stories of abortion and the desire to euthanize disabled kids because I feel guilty?
That I want to be on the same side; the side that sees me, sees
myself as the enemy? I don't know, but some people should die.

I SIT ASTRIDE RINGO, towering over Caxm, with everything in Its right place. Lupina, Pax, Michael, Jaden, and Charlotte are weaponless and in our custody. The dangerous soldiers have been whittled down, and while I have less manpower, I have Mark and his vengeful hate to scare everyone in line. Still I must be equitable and fair, even if it is just for show.

The Battle of Caxm is over, and with the unknowing and unnerving help of Mark being mistaken for Kevin, we won. I am still in charge.

The captives sit defeated on the ground before me. They are surrounded by the remaining soldiers and ringed by the rest of Caxm, still unarmed and in shock. A pile of dead bodies lay in a heap, covered by a tarp, under an apple tree. Fetty isn't in the pile, yet.

She is laying on her back with her head in Lupina's lap. Writhing in pain, her legs and arms make palsied movements as Charlotte tries to comfort her and Lupina focuses on disinfecting Fetty's once beautiful face. Her left eye has been blown out. A vicious gouge runs from it, scalding a bloodied canyon through her kinky hair. Shrapnel has pock-marked the left side of her face, leaving notches in her ear, a hole in her cheek.

Fetty, in her vicious tempo and temper, shot a soldier in the act of throwing a grenade. He dropped it as he fell dead, and right when Fetty ran passed him, the explosion took her down.

It's moot, anyway.

"Tomorrow, at sunrise, we will have a trial," I tell the criminals and the crowd. "For your crimes of attacking Caxm, for your crime..." I focus on Pax. "...of killing Kevin, you will be tried. And if found guilty, you will be executed."

I continue to stare down Pax. But he just gapes out, like a broken man, past Ringo's legs to the trees in the distance. I need to get his attention for this to work the way I want, to get him to confess to save Lupina's life.

"However, if it is found out that not all of you participated in the attack equally, if some of you were forced to go along, your lives may be spared."

With this, Pax glances up at me, then to Lupina, covered in blood and caring for a woman who just received a death sentence.

Lupina looks up from her care, from the blood and iodine drenched bandages across Fetty's face. She gives me a hard, killer stare. I realize we are near the spot that Fetty pulled me down from Ringo and gave me a similar glare.

"I will represent us in your *trial*," she says. "And I will share the same fate as everyone else."

8

THE TRIAL

~

Throughout the imprisonment of the ones who attacked Caxm, throughout my speech about the trial and plans for execution, Mark remained silent, like some overseer, some boss who will let kids play a game as long as it ends in his favor, like an ultra-rich person who will let political parties fight and squabble as long as they remain in power, in control.

He holds his rifle. His index finger sliding along the trigger guard. He continuously scans everyone like he is coordinating a symphony of kills to be orchestrated as soon as shit goes wrong.

He is like Kevin in many ways, but in truth, he seems to be what Kevin would have turned into, an unfeeling killing machine addicted to the violence, similar to Fetty's metamorphosis from a shy girl to a huntress of men.

I look to her, sitting on a one of the benches of the accused. Half her head is wrapped in bandages, still wet and stained brownish red. She isn't scanning the crowd; she watches me constantly with her one good eye open, watering, strained with overuse. Like Mark, she is planning death.

The rest of the accused sit, arms tied, on the benches. Pax looks lost and sullen, again, and cowers under Mark's presence. Michael too, ashamed at his failure to stop me, his failure to be the big man he always thought he was, sits defeated and silent on the bench, weighed down with averageness and mediocrity. Jaden and Charlotte seem to have found comfort in each other and tangle their tied hands together.

Only Lupina, their advocate, a defender for all, is unobstructed by shackles. We are letting her walk, talk without bonded hands as another measure of our fairness, and because she is no danger. Not like Fetty, who on top of hands tied and eye comprised, has her feet bound to the bench. Pax too, shifty fuck.

Another example of our fairness: there are three judges that will decide, by majority vote, the guilt or innocence, blond-beard, Spencer, and myself. Mark isn't part of Caxm, but I'm sure he will execute Pax no matter what we decide. Regardless, everyone knows how the soldier and I will vote.

"We have two crimes." I start. "There is the murder of seven guards of Caxm, carried out by Pax and Fetty, but at your request, Lupina, you are all being charged as accessories. And there is the charge of murdering one of our own, Kevin Curtis, for which, at this time, only Pax is on trial."

"Don't do this," Pax whispers to Lupina.

Lupina turns around, her back to me. I think she is going to speak to Pax, but she addresses the whole village. Behind the accused sit all of the teenagers who fled to Caxm. Surrounding them, filling in the spaces between the trees, squatting on their heels like extras in a third world country film, sit the original villagers. They can't understand the proceedings but they watch with silent interest.

I actually side with Pax on not trying the group for his and Fetty's crimes. I don't think Caxm has the stomach to watch Lupina, Charlotte, and Jaden be executed. Or even Michael, after we all just stood and watched him get whipped months before.

Lupina starts, with a voice loud and powerful. "We all took an oath, all but Kevin, all but the soldiers that Eva let take over our village. We live in a lawless land, and that is our only law. The Tribe of Iodine Wine, we swore to protect each other."

She turns back and faces me and the other judges.

"There is no murder in battle," she declares to us. This is not the tact I thought soft-spoken Lupina would take. "These soldiers are the ones that killed Sam. These soldiers are the ones that raped, murdered, and ate—yes, ate—many of our fellow teenagers who were left on the base after we escaped."

I hear an audible heave from Spencer next to me. Is this true? Did these soldiers literally feed on the teenagers? I could spin the kid's fate as not our concern, but rape and cannibalism. Fuck. No wonder the soldiers felt such shame and never wanted to go back to the base.

The crowd of Caxm unarmed and subdued until now are up and yelling, screaming at the remaining soldiers, screaming at me. Because of the attack, our numbers dwindled. I didn't think it was a big deal because we had Mark and the women, but now, after this, whose side will they be on? We all, the soldiers and judges and Mark's group, watch the crowd with fear. This could get out of hand and very bloody.

"The only crime regarding the soldiers was to let these slavers and cannibals into Caxm, and for that, Eva, you are guilty!" Lupina says.

"Is this true?" I turn to blond beard.

He shrugs. "Fuck 'em. And fuck y—"

Before he can pull his pistol, shots are fired. A cacophony of little explosions right behind my ear. I expect Mark is keeping his promise of killing *all parties involved*, filling out his decades destiny by marking off the whole goddamn rosary. I put my hand on my pistol and turn, expecting to see Mark ready to kill me.

Instead, Spriha and Joni are the ones marking notches. So quiet and timid, I thought they were no threat, even with their worn guns. But my head moves back and forth. I look to my soldiers, and they are all dead. I look back to the women, and they have stopped firing.

Mark, however, has his gun trained on Pax.

Lupina, so composed and put-together before, is panicked. A look of terror covers her face as she tries to block Pax from Mark's gun. Her hands are up, pleading with Mark and his marked-up rosary.

"No, please Mark, please don't. I know what you must fe—"

"You don't know shit," he yells. "Pax! Did you kill my son? Did you?"

"I did."

Everyone goes quiet. Even the birds that gathered after the shots were fired, that were hushed away after The Battle of Caxm to squawks and protests, are silent. They had just returned to pick on the freshly killed soldiers, so persistent that we had to cover the bodies with tarps. But even they seem to sense the silence surrounding Caxm and watch with morbid curiosity.

"Please move, Lupina. I don't want to kill you, too, but I will."

"Mark, please listen to me. Listen. Pax didn't kill Kevin, not really."

"Then who did?"

"You did. You and Bray did."

9

ANHEDONIA

~

P *ax,*

IT SEEMS, *for all my daring talents and my killer instinct, I am unable to pull my own trigger. Maybe it's the certainty of suicide that I cannot bring myself to complete; maybe, I like the odds, the small sliver of hope, that if I played counting coup I could keep playing. I want to die, but I want to live at the same time. So instead of shooting myself, I would shoot cops with paintballs or shoot drugs into my arm or constantly shoot you down, telling you lies in a dangerous setting. Please know, Lupina never told me anything. I also know the other base was sending their teenagers after us. You saw what you thought you saw and did what you said you did.*

These games, these chances of taunting death were the only forms of pleasure I could enjoy. Sad, really, to watch Michael brag about sex, to watch you and Lupina fall in love, to see Todd, faced with a much worse fate than me, still have so much joy. I know that no matter what path my life would take, I could be a famous rock musician spreading my art to millions of adoring fans, I could raise a large army and ride Bucephalus to the banks of the Indus river, and I would still find no pleasure; I would still hate myself.

I've looked back at my life in these final, crazy days of raising that army, and having those adoring fans and still felt nothing. In looking over my whole life, I tried to find moments of unknown pleasure, moments of happiness. And they seem to be stolen, a spectator of the people around me who could feel, like friends I could admire and envy, friends that I would only put in danger and envelop in my darkness. Closer, still, I would look to my family for any moments of love, any bliss. In all my recollection, I do not remember my mother ever giving me love. For show, she would throw birthday parties; she would attend school functions, until my epileptic fits made it too embarrassing. But I don't remember being cuddled, being hugged, or kissed. I never heard the words 'I love you.' It seems silly, whiney, but I can't help but think that some of my inability to feel normal pleasure was due to never being shown how.

My dad, so checked-out during the early years, and even after Bray died, tried. He took me on adventures, he taught me many things, but never taught me how to love myself, never made up for the woman he decided to marry, the woman who lacked because I lacked.

But, there is a darkness within me, always within me, that no outside circumstance or people could fix, and in a way, would only spread like a disease. Know that and do not blame yourself for what became of me.

Also, Lupina is everything I would ever want in a woman, a mother or wife, a sister or friend. My biggest regret in my short life isn't that I tricked you into killing me. This world is an ugly place, and you need to be tougher. You need to grow up. No, my biggest regret is taking you from your love, keeping you from the pleasure I could never have.

I marked her location on this map—follow the stars—the key constellation I drew has the same symbol Todd and I used in our App-

it-Tight for Destruction program. She should be where the stars are pointing. Find your way back, make up for my sins and shortcomings. And love.

Kevin

LUPINA STOPS READING, and focuses her warm eyes on Mark with sympathy, crazy considering he just threatened to kill Pax and her minutes before.

Mark just stands there, staring at the map, broken, blank faced; his gun is slack and points at the ground. His face turns white, almost devoid of life.

I wonder, now, if this my chance to disarm him, but Spriha and Joni, now lethal as hell, are watching over the reading like the true judges.

For the sake of due diligence, I assert my importance by going over to the map, taking it from Lupina and looking it over. The words seem to match what Lupina read.

"Is this his handwriting?" I clinically ask Mark.

A slight nod breaks through his stare.

I flip the paper over, to the map side. Kevin drew lots of little dark pictures across the topography, constellations connected by little stars. There is a crow, a mountain, a doorway leading to an unknown; there's even an angel, our school mascot, with a dazzling halo of light. Piercing the upright halo is the letter A.

I try to find our location on the map and know it is somewhere near the angel, but I can't place it exactly.

"What's the symbol?" I ask the group of prisoners, still shackled on the bench.

"Anarchy," Michael says. "His symbol was anarchy." He looks up at me, and he no longer looks defeated. He no longer looks like a scared boy. He looks angry.

He stands up tall. We never tied his feet to the bench. His

hands are still shackled, but the look on his face, like he is only seeing red, tells me it doesn't matter.

I take a step back and put my hand on my pistol. I wonder if David is still on my side, if the women who shot the soldiers have a dog in this fight.

"You put Anahita and our tribes in danger," Michael says.

I am about to respond, to come up with some witty retort and twisting of logic about survival of the fittest, but Michael shows me his fitness. He launches at me while breaking the cords that tie his hands.

Then he manhandles me. He twists me, turns me, and all of a sudden, I am on the ground with my arms pinned while he sits on top of me. I cannot move; I can barely breathe. He leans over, and it feels like his sit bones are going to break my ribs.

Michael picks up the map and nonchalantly reads it like an old-timer with a Sunday newspaper. "Here we are," he says. "Caxm." From my peripheral I see him point to the top of the map, above the angel, to the A in the halo.

"Home," he says.

IN THE COMMOTION of Michael pretzeling me, Spriha and Joni stopped watching Mark. I look to them for some kind of female solidarity, but they are only staring at me, pancaked on the ground, with big smirks on their faces. They are whispering shit back and forth and don't pay attention to Mark. He has removed a pistol while going behind them. His rifle is balanced with his other hand, and he points both weapons at the ladies.

"Drop your guns," he says, cold and Kevin-like.

"Mark, don't do this," Joni says.

"No one moves!" he yells. "And you two drop your weapons, now."

They have seen enough of Mark's kills to know he means business, and they put their guns on the ground.

"Now, go over there to the bench."

He marches them over toward us. I want to reach for my pistol but can't. Hell, I even want Michael to do it. Does he understand what vengeance, what old, revenge bloodlust is coming our way? He is probably going to kill us all like he promised. Maybe, despite the suicide note from Kevin, he blames us all for not keeping his boy safe.

The women kneel down behind Michael and me. Lupina is on Pax's lap like a child wanting to protect their parent. Her legs are cuddled up on his legs to protect and cover as much of his body as she can.

Mark raises the pistol, and gasps flow from the crowd. He fires, multiple shots, but his arm is only at a 45-degree angle.

I turn my head, needing to witness the damage, the carnage of our past coming to catch us. The shots are aimed at Pax's spread feet. In between, the bullets cut through the rope.

Lupina, and everyone else is screaming or crying, but Pax looks calm. While soothing Lupina, he breaks his legs apart.

"Pax, you have two choices," Mark says. "You can come with me into the forest or you can watch me kill Lupina and all your friends and then die."

Pax wriggles back and forth and slides Lupina to the ground. She is crying, wailing, screaming "No!" over and over.

But he just steps over her, steps past us all and walks into the forest with Mark following.

MICHAEL HAS DISARMED me and let me go. Everyone else is cut free, and we look to Fetty to pick up one of the guns Spriha and Joni dropped.

"Take the weapon," I say. "Save him."
Lupina, still crying and thrashing on the ground, stops and looks up at her with pleading eyes.

Fetty stands up. She seems queasy, swaying back and forth. She looks toward the guns with her one good eye. And then a rifle shot rings out from the forest, crashing over Caxm like a tidal wave.

10

A HOLE IN THE EARTH

~

Everyone is here. Annie and Paco's clan came down from the high mountain meadows. The original villagers have gathered. Their kin, the tribe from Afghanistan, arrived a couple of days after. Fetty said something when they met at their village near the Panj about destroying the base, so they came up in their trucks to check it out and pick through the scraps. Loading the teenagers into their pickups and newly acquired Humvees, they rescued and brought them to Caxm. The kids, half-starved with sunken faces, now sleep in the yurts, under the villagers' care, to recover, to be fed and nursed back to health while everyone else sleeps under tarps and lean-tos despite the increasing cold. I have been sequestered in the chapel, sheltered, by myself but with hands tied.

Well, not totally alone. Under guard, Mark is with me, too. He was laid out on a hospital bed made from benches. His right shoulder is a mess of blood and iodine, local balms and bandages. Lily, from close range, shot him straight through the right rotator cuff when he was marching Pax to his execution.

After the shot rang out, she escorted Pax back to us but left Mark bleeding in the forest. Everyone was shocked, silent as they walked back into Caxm.

Finally, I asked, "Did you kill him?"

Lily only shrugged. "He might die," she said then followed it with, "Fucker should have taught his son how to respect women."

She was here since the Battle of Caxm, spying on us the whole time, waiting for her moment to strike.

Coming up with the Afghanis, Becky and Kelly joined us, too. Becky is helping coordinate the rescue and care of the lost teenagers. Kelly is recovering with them.

UNDER THEIR WATCH, from the chapel, I hear a commotion outside. It sounds like a weird menagerie of multiple languages being spoken. I am picking up some Spanish and Tajiki words in the mix. I try to focus on the English, but it is too faint.

Finally, Lupina pulls back the flaps on the yurt. She is followed by a couple of Afghani tribesmen, armed and silent. Without instruction, they go over to Mark's cot and lift him up and carry him out.

"Come outside, please," Lupina says to me.

"What's going on?"

"Your fate…it's been decided."

I look around for any delay, any weapon, or hope I can find to put off the inevitable, but I have no possessions, no friends, no chance. I am going to be executed like I wanted Pax and Fetty to be executed.

I make way out of the yurt followed by Lupina, and everyone is watching me, our tribe of Mixed/Mexican/Mormons; the women, Lily, Becky, and Kelly, who I thought I was selling into sexual slavery; the hardened Afghani soldiers; the teenagers from the base, the ones strong enough to stand; and the original villagers.

Leading them all, Anahita, comes up to me in her slow, struggling walk. Her back is twisted and turned making her look even smaller. But she comes right up to me, stands up straight, wrenches her her back, pulling her hijab back exposing a wool hat underneath, inlaid with jewels. She points her crooked little finger at me.

"You bad person; you go away," she says.

"Yasss, Queen," Charlotte says and everyone laughs. Everyone but me.

Mark is being loaded onto a truck, one of the many that came up from Afghanistan. I am to join him in exile escorted by the Afghanis. They start to walk me that way, when I stop. My highest hope was I could join Annie and Paco's clan, the path I should have originally chosen. But it's too late. Annie even joked about it, in her smart, cynical fashion, when she saw me and heard what happened. "It's not so much that women should 'lean in', it's that *everyone* should lean the fuck out."

Lupina comes and pulls me by the elbow.

"No," I say. I don't want to go away so empty. With absolutely nothing to my name, with no connection to anyone, I feel I will evaporate into nothing.

"You don't have a choice, Eva," Lupina says.

I should feel grateful at their mercy, that I am not being sentenced to death. They are showing me more leniency than I showed them.

But, as a choice, I feel like death is better than absolute banishment. Maybe this was Kevin's dilemma; so smart, so alone and unfeeling, he was reckless because he had no connection to the happiness of the people around him. And when I was in charge, at least I had a connection.

"I'd rather die than be alone."

"Killing you is too easy," Lily says.

"Think of this way," Becky says. "All you've ever aspired to, all you ever wanted, was to be in control. You didn't want to be a scholar, an athlete, an artist. You just wanted to put other women down. Pfft."

"Please, just let me keep Ringo. Please, please, please." I beg Lupina.

She looks to Fetty and smiles. Fetty nods back.

"It's a long road back," Lupina says.

"Yes…yes, it is," Fetty says. "She could use the wilderness training, learn how to sleep with one eye open, ha."

A PROCESSION of us are making our way through the forest. We went over the mountain crest and are on the road we took to get to the valley and Caxm months before. Ringo, loaded light with gear and able footed, made it over the pass with my coaxing.

Leading us down the road are Fetty and Pax, with Michael and Lupina. Fetty's bandages have dwindled but she is still a mess. Michael walks by her side. I hear him whisper sweet nothings about her beauty. A smile breaks though Fetty's hardened and battered face.

Charlotte and Jaden, Annie and Paco, are also on this excursion, along with scores of tribespeople from Caxm and Afghanistan. They have other horses and donkeys loaded up with supplies shuttled up from the destroyed base. Everyone from our original tribe, well, everyone, except me, will return to Caxm after we're done today. Ringo and I will be joining tribesmen on their long walk through Badakhshan to the Panj river in the Wakhan Valley.

Before we start the tortuous journey through the high desert, we have one more stop. We wait on the road, near the bridge we burned, replenishing our water and snacking on the wonderful bounty of Caxm. I pull succulent grasses from near the river and feed them to Ringo, cooing her with pets and kisses.

Finally, a lone Toyota truck comes over the hills, crosses the skeletal bridge and joins us. The other vehicles will take the fast way back to Afghanistan. But this truck makes a stop in front of us.

Mark is in the back.

Michael and Jaden go over to the pickup. Like pallbearers, they pull his stretcher out, right it, then follow Pax and Fetty into the forest. Mark looks catatonic, leaning back on the cot at a 45-degree angle, staring up into nothingness. His wounds are starting to heal, but he is dead inside.

We make our way through the burned forest. The charred remains of trees, misshapen and tilting, look like large, blackened tombstones from a bygone era of giants and trolls.

Pax and Fetty lead us to a clearing. The fire has turned the ground black but little, green shoots press their way up through the soot, stronger, healthier from feeding off the ash rich soil.

Between the smattering of green, there is a dead body, decayed and wasting away. We stop and stare for a long time. Mark, too, has finally come out of his stupor and looks at his son while tears stream down his face. He wriggles himself up from the stretcher, ignoring the pain in his destroyed shoulder. He stumbles and crawls, putting down his left hand for balance. Dirt and ash float up as his knees shuffle across the ground, toward Kevin.

Michael and Jaden start to dig a hole in the earth. One of many we have made, pock-marking the land like a plague, since the ground opened up and let out its chthonic toxins. I start to feel a deep, burning hate for being here, for being turned into the type of person exiled from friends. For turning Kevin into the ground, Fetty into a killer, and Michael, Pax, and Mark into broken men. I want someone to blame for my mistakes, our mistakes, and the people we've become. I think about what Kevin told me in secret, the rumors that the government was behind the catastrophe. I want to ask the others about this; maybe, I could reconnect with my tribe, try to find a common bond, a common enemy to fight against, but they would see through me; they wouldn't believe me, and we are about to bury the only other person who knows about the conspiracy.

So, I promise myself, I promise Kevin and his father and my former friends, that my price for surviving what I did, for surviving into the ugly person I became, is to find out who opened a hole in the earth, who let this evil back into the air. Yes, find out —then exact our revenge.

But for now, I focus my gaze on Mark. He is near Kevin and picks up his withered, leathered body, crumbling and too far decayed. Ash and dirt sheds from him, covering the nascent grasses dark. And with his one good arm, he tries to embrace his lost, little boy.

EPILOGUE

THE MURDER

S he thinks she is invisible, the huntress, freshly cleaned in the river and buried underneath a bristling bush of camouflage, unscented and scrubbed, waiting without movement for hours at a time on the exit paths of men and deer, waiting for the right time, for the herds of followers to stumble into the slaughter.

I love it when she kills the men best. When she drops one soldier she stays frozen, under her bush, waiting for the other scared men to whimper and yell and fire their impotent guns at ghosts. The single snap of a gunshot by a hidden girl is far more terrifying than a symphony of firepower from a bunch of men. And eventually they always scatter like leaves in the breeze, so scared of the solitary shot that they leave the body. They tried to rescue the fallen comrade once, and she left three more in her stead. Now they are too frightened to do the honorable thing, die for country or comrade.

But some of my comrades already know the drill and fly off when a man drops. If a deer falls, we wait for her to sneak out from the bush and cut the prey open, discard the juicy offal for us to devour while she is still doing her work. But she leaves the men to rot whole! What a waste, for her, but we don't mind. My friends fly off to get more friends while I work on the eyeballs. I love eyeballs, and tongue.

She stays, though, while the wolves come in and tear into the body. She watches, never leaving her nest for hours, just in case the frightened soldiers are hiding over hills, waiting for her, waiting for a chance to see movement they can shoot at. She stays, forever watching with one eye open under the bush and darkness.

NOTES

2. The Watcher

1. *Eva later claimed that she timed going to the base with Fetty sneaking in at the same time. That she was knowingly giving Fetty the distraction she needed to get into the base. This could not be corroborated by Fetty or anyone else.*

3. Cutthroat

1. *For years, Eva maintained that she never said this. She claimed she was only trying to bring peace between the valley and the base. I wasn't in Caxm at the time, but after many interviews with primary witnesses, this is the closest I could come to what really happened. Based on these first-hand observations, and the fact that Eva's story changed, this is the final version of the truth.*

ACKNOWLEDGMENTS

~

Thank you Marisa, Jenna, and Lynda for the editing and keen eyes. And Brigitte, for ignoring my "concepts" and designing a stunning cover.

The support from family and friends has been one of the best parts of writing. Thank you, wonderful Anna, for being a great writer's assistant. And thanks to my mom, Alice, for inspiring so many Huff Puff stories.

ABOUT THE AUTHOR

Brian Pacini is a native of Colorado and enjoys traveling and long bikepacking trips through the mountains and deserts.

The Queen of What Remains is his second novel, and he plans on publishing the third and final installment of the *Decades* series before the 2020 election.

He lives in Denver with his family.
www.iodinewine.com

 facebook.com/paxpacini

 instagram.com/paxpacini

www.ingramcontent.com/pod-product-compliance
Lightning Source LLC
Chambersburg PA
CBHW020101180626
46812CB00006B/2427